D1603265

DOUGLAS & McINTYRE FICTION

Fire Eyes *by D. F. Bailey*
From the Belly of a Flying Whale *by Byrna Barclay*
Zero Avenue *by Leona Gom*
The Saxophone Winter *by Robert Harlow*
The Watery Part of the World *by Gladys Hindmarch*
Crossings *by Betty Lambert*
Disappearing Moon Cafe *by Sharon Lee*
Hear Us O Lord from Heaven Thy Dwelling Place
by Malcolm Lowry
October Ferry to Gabriola *by Malcolm Lowry*
Midnight Twilight Tourist Zone *by Sharon Riis*
The True Story of Ida Johnson *by Sharon Riis*
Tears in a Glass Eye *by Kevin Roberts*
North of the Battle *by Merna Summers*

BOOKS BY W. D. VALGARDSON

Fiction

Bloodflowers
Gentle Sinners
God Is Not a Fish Inspector
Red Dust

Poetry

The Carpenter of Dreams
In the Gutting Shed

WHAT CAN'T BE CHANGED
SHOULDN'T BE
MOURNED

Short Stories

W. D. VALGARDSON

Douglas & McIntyre
Vancouver/Toronto

Douglas & McIntyre
1615 Venables Street
Vancouver, British Columbia V5L 2H1

Canadian Cataloguing in Publication Data
Valgardson, W. D.
    What can't be changed shouldn't be mourned
    ISBN 0-88894-689-9
    I. Title.
PS8593.A53W41990   C813'.54   C90-091068-2

69028

Design by Verna Wong
Cover photograph by Doane Gregory
Typeset by The Typeworks
Printed and bound in Canada by D. W. Friesen & Sons Ltd.
Printed on acid-free paper ∞

All of the characters and experiences depicted in this book are fictional.

"A Matter of Balance" was the first prize winner in the CBC annual literary
competition and was broadcast on CBC Radio. "The Cave" was first published in
Border Crossings, "Snow" in *The Malahat Review*, "Identities" in *Canadian
Short Fiction Anthology* Vol. 2, "The Couch" in *The Saturday Evening Post*,
"Saturday Climbing" in *Chatelaine* and *Rainshadow: Stories from Vancouver
Island*, "Waiting" in *Lorberg-Heimskringla*.

To Dale Valgardson

(1943–1973)

Contents

WHAT CAN'T BE CHANGED
SHOULDN'T BE
MOURNED

The Man Who Was Always Running Out of Toilet Paper

My mother's brother, Alec, confronted by stupidity or injustice beyond his comprehension, would ride his white mare into the northeast corner of his farm. There, in a grove of scrub oak, with one hand wrapped in his horse's mane and the other around a whiskey bottle, he'd lecture God.

Although, or perhaps because, he was a bachelor, he always had us over on Sundays after church. My mother would bring lunch in a picnic basket. Alec cooked supper.

Sunday was a ritual. We'd arrive still imprisoned in our good clothes, reeking of mothballs and virtue. Alec would hand my father a homemade beer. There was always a pitcher of cider for us kids. My mother had a delicate stomach, and for her, he made rose hip tea in a china teapot. His cupboard was a mishmash of mugs picked up at gas stations or through the mail, and they said things like North of Fifty-Four or Campbell's Soup. However, he had purchased one belleek cup and saucer from Eaton's. It was in this fragile bone china that he served my mother a pale, nearly transparent liquid with just a touch of honey.

He lived in an old-style prairie house, two storeys high, narrow, with a steep peaked roof. It had two front doors, one above the other. The first door was at ground level, but the second door was directly above it and opened out from his bedroom. There were no stairs, no balcony, from this second exit, just a flat clapboard wall and a door that opened into thin air. When asked about it, my mother said that it was his door to heaven, and the day Alec died, he'd step through it into God's hands. Alec said it was there because the local carpenter, when hired to build a two-storey house, used the same floor plans for both levels and didn't have enough brains to leave the door out.

In Alec's new bathroom of white tiles and gleaming porcelain (he had the first indoor plumbing in the municipality), the toilet roll holder often sat empty. When my mother, with a touch of exasperation, would mention this, Alec would say he'd just run out and promise to buy some the next time he was at the Co-op. He was thrifty—some said miserly—and besides keeping his own garden so that he could lay down pickles and relishes and fill his root cellar with cabbages and carrots and potatoes, he sought every way he could to economize. Besides his work clothes, he owned one suit and one white shirt and, as far as I know, never took a holiday. Because of his early days on the prairies, he was also a political radical.

Under the wash basin in the bathroom there was a wicker basket. Here, his thrift and his political views came together in an unexpected way. The basket was filled to overflowing with advertisements exhorting the reader to buy things such as aluminum windows, a new furnace or an encyclopedia. There were endless letters asking for donations. These ads were his substitute for the missing roll of tissue. Because of the high quality of the paper, it frequently plugged the toilet, but Alec never complained. He just took out his snake, and while I and my brothers and sisters watched, fascinated, he cleared the pipes. This stock of pamphlets was always being renewed, because if he saw something advertised that promised to make him wealthier, happier or healthier, Alec automatically wrote a letter requesting information. According to the postmaster, my uncle got more mail than anyone else in the district.

Although there were always lots of political brochures (every year he faithfully sent a dollar to each political party and, in response, received an endless supply of information and solicitations), his political radicalism revealed no particular bias. Occasionally, he had a kind word for Tommy Douglas and the CCF. What he had to say about the NDP, the Grits and the Tories was too slanderous to repeat.

The result of all this reading and discussion was that by the time I was in grade three I was able to astound my teachers by knowing the names of the different political parties and their

platforms. Once, when I asked my uncle how he voted, he out-
raged my mother by telling me that if he ever voted, his choice
would be based upon the absorbent qualities of the paper each
party sent. The slicker the paper, he maintained, the less the
party was to be trusted.

Prominent in this pile were brochures and letters from religious organizations, begging or demanding money. During the
years of our visits, I became an expert in the many devices that
can be used to part the guilty, the weak, the sick, the fearful, the
elderly and the ignorant from their savings. In third-year psycho-
logy, I wrote a paper on the emotional component of fund raising
and called it "The Evangelism of the Dollar." I received an *A* and
an offer of a job from the college alumni association.

He was, as I said, a strange man, morose and brooding, dark-
complexioned, dark-minded, fiercely argumentative about politics, religion and economics, but he hardly ever talked about
himself. Once, late in the evening after half a dozen homemade
beers, he claimed to be without any ambition except one, and
that was to nail a banker to every hydro pole lining his property.
Since the circumference of his property was four miles, if he had
ever been granted his wish, bankers in the Interlake would have
become as scarce as bobcats.

That night, as she was washing my hair, my mother explained
(we still did not have waterworks and having our weekly bath at
Alec's place on Sundays saved hauling water and heating it on
the stove—an enormous, time-consuming chore when you have
five children) that during the Depression, the bank had fore-
closed on their parents' property, and in spite of the fact that the
farm lay abandoned and all of them homeless, the bank manager
would not let the family stay in the house or plant a crop. Although she was only thirteen, my mother was forced to move to
Winnipeg and work as a domestic. What she remembered most
about the time was how terribly hard she had to work and how,
sick with fear and loneliness, she spent many nights locked in
the bathroom, crying and throwing up. Her wages, small as they
were, she sent to her parents. Alec was seventeen. He'd been
planning on taking a course in agriculture. Instead, he was
forced to leave home and he spent the next few years shuttling
back and forth across Canada, riding the rods, struggling for a

day's pay, stealing from gardens, even begging, before he found a job in the mines and earned enough to eventually buy another farm.

When anyone would come out of the bathroom, Alec would yell, even if we were in the middle of our supper—he was prone to yelling as a form of communication—"Well, what did you learn in the last fifteen minutes?" And then we'd be at it. For hours, we'd argue the politics or religion or financial information that someone had read. The walls of his house were lined with books, and as we argued, sometimes half a dozen of us or more—anyone who wanted company felt free to drop by—he'd pull books from their shelves, flip them open and astound us with facts. What subject was debated on any given evening depended upon how many visitors went to the bathroom. We might be in the middle of an argument about freight rates and the subjugation of the western provinces by eastern interests when the toilet would flush, the door would open and my uncle would shout, "Well, what did the friends of the common man offer you today?" and we'd be off on another track.

The arguments never really ended but twisted and turned, were temporarily stopped, then started again. Some arguments went on for years, with new proofs, new opinions, with the participants sometimes changing sides, then changing back again. Driven by frustration and rage—I was not allowed to stay out of the arguments but, at the same time, was unable to out-argue my uncle—I'd hunt for sources that would support my opinion. The local library with its mix of nearly unreadable classics (Sir Walter Scott) and trash (cowboy paperbacks) was of little help, and Alec would not let anyone touch his books. However, he never locked his doors, and sometimes, in desperation, when I knew he was working in the fields or shopping in town, I would sneak in and read voraciously, both eyes on the page and both ears tuned to the sound of a tractor or truck coming into the yard. If he caught me in the house, I'd pretend to be on an errand or to have come to ask his advice. At first, my surreptitious reading was not as great a help as I had hoped. While I learned to read at great speed, I did not retain the complex arguments and examples. Desperately, I began to write down important points, summarizing long material that I then could memorize in the safety of my room.

A pamphlet declaring that happiness could be achieved by applying for a loan to purchase a new car led to a labyrinth made of interest rates, usury and the Bible. In the city to help my father sell freshly killed chickens door to door (they'd quit laying and soon would be so tough they could be chewed only by a young bear), I flung myself into a secondhand bookstore where for fifty cents apiece I was able to get an economics textbook and a set of interest tables. The proprietor tried to sell me a novel about children spending their summer at the cottage (I was thirteen), then seeing that I was adamant about usury, told me to try the public library and gave me its address. It took me three weekend trips to figure out how to use the card catalogue, and at first, I was overwhelmed by too many books. The arguments, in the meantime, ranged far and wide, but I had a bone I was determined to chew. I secretly coveted a red convertible and already planned, the moment I finished school, to get a job with the Highways Department and to spend my meagre savings as a down payment on just such a vehicle. At night, I lay awake for hours rehearsing how I would drive down Main Street and bask in everyone's admiration, and I wasn't going to let anyone get away with saying that buying a car on time was a sucker's game.

The only one Alec did not attack was my mother. Anyone else expressing an opinion, no matter how dearly held, would be challenged with "Where's the proof?" Proof became the centre of my life. Every time I opened my mouth, I had three examples to back up my opinion.

One Sunday, my mother said to one of my younger brothers, "Drink your milk, it's good for you."

Before the last word had died, I jumped out of my chair and demanded, "Where's your proof?"

Stung that women's wisdom passed down the centuries should be publicly challenged, she answered, "It builds bones. And teeth."

"Strontium 90," I shot back.

For the next month, she wouldn't serve me anything with milk in it. Rice pudding, chocolate pie, ice cream—my portions all were divided up among my brothers and sisters. As a mother, Alec said, she had many virtues, but she was not as open-minded as she might have been. He also read me a description of the trial and death of Socrates.

I feel Alec sometimes planted certain papers at the top of the pile. Why else would I find letters denouncing the United Nations as a communist plot? Do you know where that can lead you? The League of Nations, the use of military conflict to settle disagreements, the formation of city-states, national pride, the military-industrial complex, balance of power and the biblical description of the final destruction of the world.

One winter evening as we struggled home through the snow, full of *peroghi* and *holobchi*, my father said, "He thinks too much. It'll be the end of him. A man like that." He shook his head as if to suggest the dire consequences of so much thought. But it didn't happen that way. Instead, water and gravity conspired to undo my uncle. Unseasonal rains had kept him out of his fields. Although he frequently rode his white horse into the oak grove to set God straight, rain continued to fall. When the sun finally appeared, Alec was in a rush to get his crops planted and started work before the ground was ready. His tractor got stuck, and when he tried to get it out, it tipped over backward and fell on him. He lay in the field for two days before our neighbours discovered his body.

That spring, his fields lay fallow. Sometimes, I'd slip through the poplar bush, over the barbed wire fence, and let myself in a back window and just sit there as if, magically, my presence would bring him noisily stamping through the back door, ready to continue our unfinished arguments. When school was out, I went to Winnipeg to work in a warehouse. In July, my parents sold Alec's house and forty acres to someone from the city who wanted it for a hobby farm.

The first thing the newcomers did was throw out all the books and put up a TV antenna. They didn't even put the books in boxes but just unloaded them at the garbage dump. I heard about it while I was eating a hamburger at Mary's Restaurant. By this time, I was eighteen and had my car (not the sleek red convertible I'd imagined but a beat-up Chevy for which I'd been able to pay cash) so I drove out to the dump. Someone had set the books on fire and they sat in a charred pile. I kicked the pile apart and salvaged what I could (117 books on everything from the lives of the saints to farming in New Guinea).

By the time his will was found, probated, everything sold, it was the end of summer. My mother got the teapot and cup and saucer, my father, the beer-making equipment and a hundred dozen bottles. The rest of the estate—every cent he'd been able to save plus the money from the farm—was to be put in trust so that my brothers and sisters and I, if we wished, could go to university. Although we all were good students, university was not something we had ever considered. Doctors' kids, lawyers' kids, city kids, they went to that mythical and rumoured place. Country kids with foreign names like Wishnowski got jobs driving trucks and shovelling gravel.

To everyone's surprise, most of all my own, in September, I found myself sitting beside the carefully tailored children of River Heights who spoke in carefully modulated voices, drove carefully chosen sports cars and skied in the Alps during Christmas break. Twice during my undergraduate years, I was asked into their homes. Although my sport jacket puckered between my shoulders and I still had difficulty remembering to put articles before nouns, I was a great hit with my classmates' fathers. I knew every advertisement their companies had ever mailed out.

After the University of Manitoba, I went to Waterloo, and from there to Harvard. Next month, I'll have my Ph.D. in political science. I've had some American job offers, but I've decided to come back to Winnipeg. I want to study the General Strike and the socio-political structure of the North End.

The committee that interviewed me for a job at the U of W asked me who had made the greatest contribution to my education. I fobbed them off with praise for one of my illustrious professors. I wonder what they would have thought if I had told them the truth—that a dark and brooding farmer who never could remember to buy toilet paper and who regularly lectured God was the best teacher I'd ever had.

A Matter of Balance

He was sitting on a cedar log, resting, absentmindedly plucking pieces from its thick layer of moss, when he first saw them. They were standing on the narrow bridge above the waterfall. When they realized he had noticed them, they laughed, looked at each other, then turned their backs. In a moment, the short, dark-haired one turned around to stare at him again. His companion flicked a cigarette into the creek.

Bikers, he thought with a mixture of contempt and fear. He had seen others like them, often a dozen at a time, muscling their way along the road. These two had their hair chopped off just above the shoulders, and from where he sat, it looked greasy and hung in tangled strands. They both had strips of red cloth tied around their heads. The dark-haired boy, he thought, then corrected himself, man, not boy, for he had to be in his middle twenties, was so short and stocky that he might have been formed from an old-fashioned beer keg. They both wore black leather vests, jeans and heavy boots.

He was sorry that they were there, but he considered their presence only a momentary annoyance. They had probably parked their bikes at the pull-off below the waterfall, walked up for God knows what reason—he could not imagine them being interested in the scenery—and would shortly leave again. He would be happy to see them go. He was still only able to work part-time and had carefully arranged his schedule so that his Wednesdays were free. He didn't want anything to interfere with the one day he had completely to himself.

The tall blond man turned, leaned against the railing and

stared up at Harold. He jabbed his companion with his elbow and laughed. Then he raised his right hand, pointed two fingers like he would a pistol and pretended to shoot.

The action, childish as it was, unsettled Harold, and he felt his stomach knot with anxiety. He wished that he were on the other side of the bridge and could simply pick up his pack and walk back to his station wagon. The only way across the river, however, was the bridge, and he had no desire to try to force his way past them. They reminded him of kids from his public school days who used to block the sidewalk, daring anyone to try to get by. He had been in grade two at the time and had not yet learned about fear. When he had attempted to ignore them and go around, they had shifted with him to the boulevard, then to the road and, finally, to the back lane. As his mother was washing off his scrapes and bruises and trying to get blood off his shirt, he had kept asking her why, why did they do it? Beyond saying that they were bad boys and that she would speak to the principal, she had had no answers. Only later, when he was much older, had he understood that their anger was not personal and, so, could not be reasoned with.

Every Wednesday for the last six months, he had hiked to the end of this trail and then used his rope to lower himself to the riverbank. Before the winter rains began and flooded the gorge, he wanted to do as much sniping as possible. The previous week, he had discovered a crack in the bedrock that looked promising, but before he had a chance to get out all the gravel, the day had started to fade and he had been forced to leave. The gorge was no place to spend the night. Even at noon, the light was filtered to a pale grey. He dressed warmly, wearing a cotton shirt, then a wool shirt and, finally, a wool jack-shirt; yet within a few hours, he was always shaking with cold. As strenuous as the panning was, it could not keep him warm. The air was so damp that when he took a handful of rotting cedar and squeezed it, red water ran like blood between his fingers. On the tree trunks, hundreds of mushrooms grew. At first, because of their small size and dark grey colour, he thought they were slugs, but then he pried one loose with his fingernail and discovered its bright yellow gills.

Although he had been nowhere near the bottom of the crack, he had found a few flakes of gold, which he meticulously picked out of his pan with tweezers. Panning in the provincial parks was illegal, so he always went right to the end of the path, then worked his way along the river for another hundred yards. Once, he had taken a quarter-ounce of dust and small nuggets out of the river and he wondered if someone had found out, but he immediately dismissed the idea. Only his psychiatrist knew. When they met each Thursday, he always showed Conklin his latest find. As far as his friends and colleagues were aware, he spent his days off hiking, getting himself back into shape after having been ill for over a year.

As he studied the two men below, he told himself he was letting his imagination run away with him again and to get it under control. There was no good in borrowing trouble. He stood up, swung his pack onto his shoulders and, being careful not to look like he was running away, resumed his hike.

From this point on, the trail was a series of switchbacks. If the two on the bridge were planning on following him and stealing his equipment or wallet, they would probably give up after a short distance and wait for easier prey. Unless they were in good condition, the steep climb would leave them gasping for breath.

Large cedars pressed close to the path, blocking out the light. Old man's beard hung from the branches. The ground was a tangle of sword fern, salal and Oregon grape. In a bit of open space, an arbutus twisted toward the sun. Its bark, deep earth-red, hung in shreds. Here and there, the new pale green bark was visible. That was the way he felt, like a snake or an arbutus, shedding his old skin for a new, better one. The previous year when nothing else had seemed to work, he had taken his pack and hiked from sunrise to sunset, exhausting himself so completely that he could not stay awake. The sniping, looking for gold in cracks, under rocks, among the roots of trees, had come when he had started to feel better.

At the next bend, he stopped and hid behind a rotting stump. In a couple of minutes his pursuers—he told himself not to be foolish, not to be paranoid—appeared. They were walking surprisingly fast. If the trail had been even slightly less steep, they would have been running.

He wished there were a cutoff that would allow him to circle back. He could, he realized, use his equipment, if necessary, to lower himself to the river, but to do so he would need to gain enough of a lead to have time to untie and uncoil the rope, to set it around a tree, to climb down and then to pull his rope down after him so that it could not be taken away or cut. He then would be faced with the problem of finding a route up. He had to be back by seven. It was the agreed-upon time. Since their mother had been killed, the children became upset if he was even a few minutes late.

He looked at his watch. It was ten o'clock. It was a two-hour hike to the end of the trail, but he could hike out in an hour and a half. That did not leave him much time. First, he wanted to clean out the crack and, if possible, begin undercutting a large rock that sat in the centre of the river. Undercutting was dangerous. It would require that he move rocks and logs to divert the shallow water to either side of where he was going to work. Then he would need more logs to prop up the rock. He didn't want to get the work partly done and have half a ton of stone roll onto him. The nuggets that might be clustered around the base were worth some risk, but there was no sense in taking more chances than necessary.

Ahead, through a gap in the trees, he saw the railway trestle. The two behind him would, he told himself, stop there. Hardly anyone went farther. The trestle was an inexplicable focal point. Every weekend, dozens of people hiked to it, then dared each other to cross over the gorge. Many, terrified of heights, balked after the first few steps and stood, rigid, unable to force themselves to go farther.

That, he reassured himself, was what those two were coming for. They would cross the trestle and scare each other by roughhousing like a couple of adolescents.

He had hoped, unreasonably, that there would be hikers or a railway crew on the tracks. Normally, it was a relief when there was no one there. Hikers were inclined to talk about their experiences, and in the past, he had been afraid that if he was frequently seen on the same trail, his weekly visits might come to the attention of the park warden. To avoid that, he had deliberately arranged to come when the park was empty.

He did not stop but crossed over the tracks and entered the forest on the far side. The path dwindled to a narrow line of crushed ferns. The trees were shagged with windblown moss and deadfall was everywhere. It was old forest, and in all the time he had come, he had never seen a bird or animal. As a child he had dreamed of living in the forest. In his dreams, his hunting had always been rewarded with game. The discrepancy between what he had hoped for and reality still astounded him.

While he was able to see the railway tracks, he stopped and waited. His legs had begun to tire and cramp. He stretched them, then kneaded his right calf with his thumb and forefinger. Always before, he had valued the silence and isolation. Now, however, as he watched the two bikers look up and down the roadbed then cross the path, Harold felt the forest close around him like a trap.

He hurried away. Even as he fled, he reassured himself that they had done nothing. Anyone was free to hike wherever he wanted. If he just stopped, they would catch up and pass him by without paying any attention to him.

He kept his eyes on the path. He had no intention of tripping over a vine or slipping on a log. His fear, he chided himself, was not rational. If a Mountie suddenly appeared and asked him what was the matter, what could he say? That he hadn't liked the way they had looked at him earlier? That they had threatened him? And how was that, sir? He could hear the question. And the answer? The blond one pointed his finger at me. Any Mountie would think him mad.

The moss was so thick that his feet made no sound. There was only the creak of his pack, the harsh sound of his breathing. He would, he decided, abandon his plans, and when he got to the end of the granite ridge that ran along on his left, he would double back through the narrow pass on its far side. People don't assault other people without good reason, he told himself, but it did no good. His panic fluttered like dry leaves in a rising wind.

He wished that he had brought a hunting knife. It would have made him feel better to have a weapon. His mind scurried over the contents of the pack as he tried to determine what he could use in a fight. The only possibility was his rack of chock nuts. It wasn't much. A dozen aluminum wedges, even clipped together on a nylon sling, would not be very effective.

As he came to the end of the ridge, he turned abruptly to the left. The pass was nearly level and, unlike the area around it, contained only a few scattered trees. There were, he remembered, circles of stones where people had made campfires. One day he had poked about and discovered used condoms, some plastic sandwich bags and four or five beer bottles. A broken beer bottle, he thought, would serve as a weapon. He was just beginning to search for one when he saw a movement at the far end of the pass.

He became absolutely still. He felt so weak that he thought he was going to fall down. He craned his neck for a better look. If there were two of them, he could circle back the other way. In a moment, he realized that there was only one. That meant the other was on the path he had just left. He spun on his heel and ran back to the fork. No more than a quarter of a mile away the path ended. At that point, there was nothing to do but return the way he had come or descend to the river. In either case, he was trapped. His mouth, he realized, was so dry he could not spit.

Behind him, he heard someone ask a question that sounded like "Where did he go?" and a muffled reply, but he could not be sure of the words. The ground was nearly level. He was running when he burst out onto an area where the rock fell from the side of the trail like a frozen set of rapids. There were few places here for trees to root. Leaves and pine needles were swept from the pale green lichen by the winter rains. Rather than continue to what he knew was a dead end, he clambered down the slope. He had not explored this area. In the back of his mind was the hope that the rough rock continued all the way to the river. By the time they found out he was no longer on the path, he could have climbed the other cliff. All at once, he stopped. The rough black rock turned into sixty feet of smooth slab.

There was no time to go back. He glanced over his shoulder, then at the slab. It was, he realized, deceptive. It angled down toward the river, then stopped at a ragged edge. No steeper than a roof at the outset, it curved just enough that every few feet the angle increased. Patches of lichen and the smooth texture of the stone guaranteed that anyone who ventured out on it would be engaged in a test of balance.

There was a chance, because of his friction boots, that he could work his way onto the steepest part of the slope. If the two behind him were not pursuing him, they would pass by and he would never see them again. If they were, for whatever reason, meaning him some harm, they would have great difficulty reaching him.

Quickly, he unzipped the right-hand pocket of his pack and pulled out a section of three-millimetre rope. He tied a figure-eight knot in both ends, wrapped the rope around his left hand, then crept down to a small evergreen. Ten feet to the right, in a completely exposed area, there was a gnarled bush. Here and there, stunted trees, their trunks nearly as hard as the rock itself, protruded from cracks.

There was little room for error. If he began to slide, it would be difficult to stop before he went over the edge. At this part of the river, the fall would not be great, but height would not make any difference. Even a twenty-foot fall onto the scattered boulders of the riverbed would certainly be fatal. He leaned out, brushed away some dust that had collected on the rock, then took his first step.

Above him, someone whistled sharply. It startled him, but he kept his eyes fixed on the surface of the rock. He fitted the toe of his boot onto a small nubbin, then his other toe onto a seam of cracked quartz. The greatest danger was that, for even a split second, he would allow himself to be distracted. For his next move, he chose a pebbled area no bigger than a silver dollar. From there, he moved to a depression that was only noticeable because of its slight shadow. He had crossed more difficult areas than this but always with the security of a harness and rope and a belayer he could trust. A fall in those circumstances meant no more than some scraped skin and injured pride.

When he was within two feet of the bush, he felt a nearly overwhelming urge to lunge forward. He forced himself to stay where he was. On the rock there could be no impetuous moves. Patience, above all else, was to be valued. There seemed to be no place for him to put his foot. He scanned the surface. Just below him there was a hairline crack. If he pressed down hard on it, it would hold him long enough for him to step to the side and up and catch hold of the bush.

Slowly, he pirouetted on his left foot, then brought his right foot behind it. He took a deep breath, forced the air out of his lungs, then in one fluid movement, stepped down, up and across.

Even as his hand grasped the wooden stem, he felt his feet begin to slide.

While he unwrapped the three-millimetre rope from his arm, he sat with his legs on either side of the stem. He fitted a loop of rope around an exposed root, then slipped the second loop around his wrist. Unless the root gave way, the farthest he was going to fall was a couple of feet.

Only then did he allow himself to look back. There was still no sign of anyone. The area of tumbled rock ran on for a fair distance and, he realized, would take a while to search. He cursed himself for not taking a chance and running back the way he had come.

He hooked his pack to the bush, took out the sling with the hardware on it, then eased himself out onto the steepest section of slab he could reach. Here he crouched, with his back to the trail, his hands splayed against the rock.

There was a sharp whistle above him. It was immediately answered from some distance back toward the trestle. With that, he realized that they had split up. One had blocked the trail while the other had done the searching.

He looked back again. Thirty feet behind him was the dark-haired biker. His blond companion was swinging down from the left. Both of them, Harold could see, were tired. He had, he thought, with a distant kind of pleasure, given them a good run for their money. If they had been carrying packs, he would have outdistanced them.

They both stopped at the rough edge, some ten feet apart, looked at each other and smirked.

"Did you want something?" he asked. He had meant to make it a casual question, even offhand, as though he had no idea they had followed him, but panic sharpened his voice.

They both laughed as if at a joke.

"What do you want?" He was no longer sure that what he had planned would work.

The blond man had a small leather purse attached to his belt. He unsnapped it and took out a bone-handled clasp knife. He pried out a wide blade.

"Are you crazy?" Harold cried. "What's the matter with you? I don't even know you."

They both grinned foolishly and studied their boots. They

looked, he thought wildly, like two little boys caught in the middle of a practical joke.

Panic made him feel like he was going to throw up. "Are you nuts?" he shouted. "Are you crazy or something?"

Their answer was to start down the slab, one on each side of him. Their first steps were confident, easy. The surface of the rock was granular and bare at the edge and provided plenty of friction. He could see that neither was experienced. They both came down sideways, leaning into the rock, one hand pressed to the surface. He gripped the nylon sling in his right hand and concentrated on keeping his balance.

The dark-haired one was closest. He was coming down between the tree and the shrub, taking little steps, moving his left foot down, then his right foot, then his left, dangerously pressing all his weight onto the edge of his boot and, even more dangerously, leaning backward, throwing off his centre of balance. Suddenly, a piece of lichen peeled away and his left foot slid out from under him. Instead of responding by bending out from the rock and pressing down with his toes, he panicked. He was sliding faster and faster. His body was rigid, his face contorted with fear, his eyes, instead of searching for a place he could stop his slide, were desperately fixed on the safe area he had just left behind. He made no sound. When he was finally even with Harold, he reached out his hand as though expecting it to be taken. There was, Harold saw, on the back of the hand, a tattoo of a heart pierced by a knife. A red and blue snake wound up the arm and disappeared beneath the sleeve. It was only by luck that his one foot struck a piece of root and he stopped. He was no more than a foot from the edge.

The blond man had come at an angle, picking his way along by fitting his knife blade into a crack. Just before his companion lost control, the blond man had started to work his way across an area where there were no cracks. He seemed frozen into place.

"Why?" Harold shouted at him.

The sound seemed to wake the blond man from a stupor. He turned his head slowly to look at Harold. He squinted and formed his mouth into a small circle, then drew his chin down and ran his tongue along his lower lip. For a moment, Harold thought the biker was going to turn and leave.

"Get me out of here," his companion cried. Fear made his voice seem as young as a child's.

The blond man shook his head, then half-snarled, stood up and tried to walk across the intervening space. It was as though momentum and will held him upright; then Harold swung the nylon sling over his head, lunged forward and struck his opponent on the upper arm. The blow was not powerful, and normally, it would have been swept aside. But here, as they both teetered on the steep surface, it was enough to knock them both off balance.

As the blond man skidded down the rock, he jabbed at it with his knife, trying to find an opening. Six feet from the edge, he managed to drive the blade into a crack. The knife held. He jammed his fingers into the crack.

Harold had slipped, fallen, then been caught by the rope around his wrist. He pulled himself back to the shrub and knelt with his knee against the stem.

"Help us up," the dark-haired man begged. He looked like he was on the verge of weeping.

Harold loosened the rope, then untied it. Carefully, giving his entire attention to the task, he retraced his original route. Once at the evergreen, he knew he was safe. His sides were soaked with sweat and he could smell his own fear, bitter as stale tobacco. The two men never stopped watching him.

When Harold reached the top of the slab, the blond man called, in a plaintive voice, "For God's sake, don't leave us here."

Fear had softened their eyes and mouths, but he knew it was only temporary. If he drew them to safety, they would return to what they had been.

"Pull us up," the dark-haired man whined. His red headband had come off and was tangled in his hair.

Around them, the forest was silent. Not a bird called, not an animal moved. The moss that covered the rock and soil, the moss that clung thickly to the tree trunks, the moss that hung in long strands from the branches, deadened everything, muted it, until there were no sharp lines, no certainties. The silence pressed upon them. Harold had, for a moment, a mad image of all three of them staying exactly as they were, growing slowly covered in moss and small ferns until they were indistinguishable from the logs and rocks except for their glittering eyes.

"Tell somebody about us," the dark-haired man asked.

The words tugged at him like little black hooks. He looked down. Their faces were bleached white with fear. He could tell someone, a park warden, perhaps, but then what would happen? If he could be certain they would be sent to prison, he might dare tell somebody, but he knew that would not happen. If charges were laid, he would have to testify. They would discover his name and address. And from then on, he would live in fear. Afraid to leave his house. Afraid to go to sleep at night. Afraid for his children. And what if they denied everything, turned it all around? He had had the necessary equipment to rescue them and had refused. What if one of them had fallen by the time someone came? He could be charged with manslaughter and the children would be left without mother or father. No matter how he tried to keep his psychiatrist out of it, Conklin would become involved. Harold knew how people thought. His short stay in hospital for depression, his weekly visits to a psychiatrist to siphon off pain and, automatically, he was crazy.

"You bastard," the blond man screamed. "You bastard. Get us out of here." He kept shifting his feet, trying to find a purchase where there was none. "If you don't, our friends will come. They'll get us out. Then we'll start looking for you. There's thousands of us. We'll find you."

The screaming startled him for a moment, but then he thought about how soon the little warmth from the sun would disappear, of how the fog would drift down with the darkness, of how the cold would creep into everything, of how few people came this way.

He wondered if his wife had screamed like that. Six of her fingernails had been broken. *Unto the third generation*, Conklin had said. His children, and his grandchildren should he have any, would feel the effects. Alone in a dark parking lot, desperately fighting for her life, and he had been sitting in his study, reading. "Help never comes when it's most needed."

Then, with real regret for the way things are, he hefted his pack so that it settled firmly between his shoulders and returned the way he had come.

Saturday Climbing

Sixty feet up the cliff, the toe of his climbing boot resting on a ledge no wider than a dime, two fingers curled around a nubbin of rock, Barry was suddenly afraid that he would fall. "Rope," he called.

At the foot of the cliff, his daughter let out the golden line of rope that joined them. As Barry felt the rope go slack, he raised his right knee and pressed his toe into a shallow depression. Grunting with the strain, he stood up on his right leg, then paused, uncertain of his next move.

The cliff had proven to be deceptive. The conglomerate, with its rough, gravel-like surface, had looked easy. Close to the base there were large handholds, so that at first the climbing was little more difficult than walking up stairs. Then, unexpectedly, the surfaces smoothed; the places where he could get a secure hold were spread farther and farther apart. At the same time, the numerous cracks dwindled until there was no place to set any protection. Unable to go back because of his pride, he had continued until he now found himself dangerously far above his last piton. If he fell, he would drop twenty-five feet to the piton, then twenty-five feet past it before his rope came taut and held him. There was, because of the elasticity of the rope, a chance that he would ground out.

The thought flitted through his mind that it would be like falling from the top of a six-storey building. Tensing his fingers, he straightened his elbow and leaned back from the rock so that he could search for his next hold. Above him, there was a half-inch ledge. He reached up, got a good grip, then lifted his left leg higher than he had ever imagined he could and set his foot on the rough patch that would provide the necessary friction to hold his weight.

He had been scared many times but never like this. Never before had he been this close to paralysis, to a sensation of letting go so that the tension and the fear would be over. The way he felt, he imagined, was the way a wounded animal felt when it finally gave up fleeing and allowed itself to be killed.

Six inches from his left hand there was a vertical crack that seemed hardly wider than a fingernail. Cautiously, he explored it with his fingers. Just within his reach it widened slightly. He ran his hand over his rack and unsnapped the smallest chock nut. He forced the aluminum wedge deep into the crack. From the wedge there hung a wire loop and from that a carabiner. Catching hold of the rope tied to his harness, he lifted it up, forced open the spring-loaded gate of the carabiner and fitted the rope into the aluminum oval.

Once the gate snapped shut, he sighed with relief. The chock nut, the wire loop, the carabiner, the rope, fragile as they looked, would hold ten times his weight. If he wanted to he could let go and simply hang in space.

"You all right?" his daughter called.

"Yeah," he lied, "just resting."

His voice sounded faint and breathy. He was glad she could not see his momentary weakness. He could not control the trembling of his legs. The muscle of his right arm jerked spasmodically. Ever since his wife had left them, he had tried to compensate by providing unhesitating leadership for his daughter. He did his best to keep life simple and uncomplicated. It was, he thought, the way to provide her with security.

He glanced down. Among the scattered grey boulders, Moira's red hair gleamed like a burnished cap.

"You're doing fine," she hollered. The crosscurrents of air that played over the cliff face blurred her voice, making it seem farther away than it really was. To hear what she said, he had to strain toward the sound. "You've got another twenty feet to a big ledge. You can do it easy."

He was grateful for her confidence. Before they had started climbing, there had crept into his daughter's voice a constant note of disparagement and disappointment. The times he had managed to overcome his own insecurity and had asked her what was the matter, she had turned her back on him, answering "Nothing" with a tightly controlled voice.

Bewildered, he had sought the advice of women at work who had teen-age daughters. They had been no help. Behind their competent, efficient professional selves, they were, he had realized, just as confused as he was. In desperation, he had gone so far as to pose to his class the question of the relationship of fathers and daughters. He had not been prepared for the reaction he got. From every corner of the room had come cries of bitter disappointment and resentment.

As he had left the classroom, one student had called to him. He had stopped to wait for her. She had frizzy dark hair, wore long dresses that might have come from a western movie set, a rainbow assortment of beads and a nose ring. She always talked as if she were thinking in some exotic language and translating it badly. She was the only student he'd ever had who insisted on analyzing *War and Peace* by consulting the *I Ching*.

"The caged bird proves nothing but the power of the captor," she had intoned.

For a moment, he suffered vertigo, and the cliff seemed to sway as if in an earthquake. He pressed his forehead to the cool stone and shut his eyes. Inside his flesh, his bones trembled.

Taking up rock climbing had been an act of desperation. All the past activities Moira and he had done together—going to foreign films, visiting Seattle, beachcombing—she had dismissed with a contemptuous shrug of her shoulders. At one time, they had played chess nearly every day. Lately, she pretended she had never seen the game. When he had noticed an advertisement for rock climbing, he remembered that she had spoken admiringly of classmates who had hiked the West Coast Trail. He had registered them and paid their fees. Then he had informed her.

He had hoped she would be pleased. Instead, she was incensed that he had committed her to something without her consent. He knew she was right to be angry but he was too frantic to care. Over the previous month, she had come home late a number of times. Each time, the sweet-sour smell of marijuana clung to her, and her pupils seemed unnaturally large. He had not dared to accuse her of smoking dope. If he was wrong, she would never forgive him for being unjust. Being right frightened him even more. If she said, "That's right. I'm smoking dope, six joints a day, and sniffing coke and participating in orgies," he didn't know what he would do. Ranting and raving had ceased to work. Reasoning with her had no effect. He felt utterly helpless.

By emphasizing that the money was spent and there was no refund, he won the argument over rock climbing. However, while he took the car to the first class, she took her bike. She went prepared to sneer at everything, but once she saw her classmates, her attitude changed. Instead of Moira being isolated by her youth, Barry was isolated because of his age. Of the fifteen members, eleven were under twenty. The instructor still didn't need to shave more than once a week.

By the time the three hours were over and he realized that rock climbing wasn't going to be rough hiking, it was too late to back out. There were only three girls in the class. In return for the attention of one-third of the young men, Moira was prepared to scale the Himalayas.

Barry began with an attitude that was typical of someone raised on the prairies. Anything over three feet was a substantial elevation. During the second class, he was expected to climb vertical cliffs. He gave some thought to dropping out of the class but realized that, after the fuss he had made about the fees, he would look like a dreadful hypocrite.

Gradually, as a dozen Saturdays passed, what had seemed impossible was reduced to the merely difficult. Cliffs that had looked flat and smooth as polished marble became a series of problems and solutions. The names of the unfamiliar equipment became a part of his vocabulary. Young men in climbing boots frequented his back yard and kitchen. To his relief, Moira accepted him enough to spend an occasional hour practising knot-tying with him.

This weekend there had been no class. In an attempt to heal a rift caused by an argument over her going away to college—she was two years ahead of herself in school and, therefore, in spite of being in grade twelve was only sixteen—he had offered to go climbing with her. To his surprise, she'd accepted.

"Climbing," he called.

"Climb on," Moira answered.

He stepped up, away from the safety of his perch. His life, he realized, was in her hands. If he fell, she was his protection.

The thought of giving her so much responsibility was like the prick of a thorn. In all other things, he had been trying to keep her from rushing headlong into taking on too much responsibility at once. The result had been a long series of disagreements. She did not have the decency to let one dispute finish before she began another. Sometimes three or four overlapped.

On Fridays, when he went to the faculty club, he ordered double brandies and brooded over whether he shouldn't have insisted on Sunday school in a good fundamentalist church all the past years. When they talked about their teen-age children, his colleagues, the majority of whom were the epitome of liberal tolerance about most things, reverted to wistful fantasies about convents and boarding schools in inaccessible locations.

The weekend past, Moira had wanted to go to an all-night party with a boy he just vaguely recognized as having drifted through the house two or three times. Barry was dumbfounded. At the same age, he'd had to have his girlfriends in before midnight. If he had kept a girl out all night, her father would have met them with a shotgun.

"Good girls," he said, quoting something he'd heard in adolescence, "don't stay out all night."

"Good fathers," she shot back, "don't think the worst of their daughters."

That afternoon was filled with slamming doors, weeping and raised voices. He found himself fighting so hard against her staying out all night that he compromised on three o'clock and afterward, when he had calmed down, wondered how it had happened. He had been determined to start with a deadline of midnight and let himself be persuaded to accept one o'clock. Although Moira claimed not to remember the chess moves, he had the distinct feeling that he'd been checkmated.

The final blow had been her insistence on going away to college. They had the money, he admitted. It just wasn't sensible, at sixteen, to travel two thousand miles to attend a school when the local university was every bit as good, even if it did have him on the faculty. He suspected the choice had more to do with her all-night party boy than with academic excellence.

Now, as he worked his way up toward the large ledge where

he was to set up a belay station, it was as if Barry were in danger of being pulled backward by the sheer weight of his memories. It was with a sense of relief that he heaved himself over the ledge. He paused to catch his breath, then anchored himself to a boulder.

"On belay," he shouted down, giving Moira the signal that he was ready.

His daughter, eighty feet below, seemed so small that Barry felt he could lift her into his arms. She looked no larger than she had when, at three, she had eaten a bottle of aspirin. He had scooped her up and run with her four blocks to the hospital. After that desperate race and the struggle to hold her down—it had taken both him and a nurse to control her flailing limbs while the doctor pumped her stomach—he was acutely aware of how tenuous her life was, of how much he would suffer if he lost her. For a long time afterward, he thought of her as being intricately constructed of fragile paper.

"Climbing," Moira answered.

"Climb on," he shouted.

From time to time, she paused to pull loose the chock nuts and pitons her father had left behind. These, since they would be needed later, she clipped to a sling that hung over her shoulder. Once, when she deviated from the route her father had taken, she became stuck at an overhang. Not having dealt with the obstacle himself, Barry could not help and had to leave her to find her own solution.

The climb seemed agonizingly slow, as if it would never be completed. Then, when it was over, and his daughter, grinning, breathless, was climbing over the edge, it was as if hardly any time had passed.

They sat side by side, sipping orange juice, their feet dangling in space.

"I thought you were in trouble," Moira said.

"I though you were too," he replied, matching his weakness with hers. Then, ashamed, he admitted, "I gripped."

Moira twisted about. Her red hair was snugged at the back with a rubber band. Being outside had sprinkled her nose with light freckles.

She studied the cliff face. It rose another hundred feet. There was a crack that ran more than halfway, then a small series of outcrops. He tried to see the route they should take, but the last ten or fifteen feet seemed impossible.

"I'd come home for Christmas," she said in a rush, "and classes are out in April. It's not as if it was such a long time to be away."

She had caught him unaware, and none of his carefully prepared arguments were at hand.

"It's just so unexpected," was all that he could manage.

"I've got to leave sometime."

The house will be so empty, he wanted to say. How will I get used to being alone? It is as if you lost your first tooth only last year. As if I took you to kindergarten six months ago. You're barely rid of your braces.

She lifted her index finger and rubbed the side of her nose. She had done it as long as he could remember. It was her signal that she was going to impart a confidence or confess a wrongdoing—that she liked some boy in her class, that she had got a detention or that she had spent all her allowance before the end of the week and needed more money.

"I'm not innocent, you know."

He wondered what she meant by that but was afraid to ask.

"I mean," she continued, "Vic High's a big school. You hear a lot. Everybody's on the pill. The dope's there if you want it. There's lots of opportunity."

He was tempted to let loose his anxiety in a lecture, but the memory of the frizzy-haired student in his class stopped him. She had stood on one foot all the time they were talking, the sole of her left sandal pressed to her right knee. She had passed her hand before his face in an affected arc. He'd heard her father was a prominent lawyer in the East but found it hard to believe.

She had talked in aphorisms and riddles, then a silence had fallen between them. He'd wondered why she had bothered to call after him, what she had really wanted to say. He had left her but, after a few steps, glanced back. She had given up her stork-like stance and was standing with feet together, shoulders slumped, her face slack beneath her gaudy makeup. For the first time, he had seen how much younger she was than he had thought. If he had not known better, he'd have said she was a lost child.

Just then, she had seen him watching her. Immediately, she had drawn up her shoulders, flung back her head, given an exaggerated sway of her hips and pranced away. That had been the last time he'd seen her. She had never come back to his class, and one day a yellow drop-slip with her name on it had appeared in his mailbox.

"I want to lead this pitch," Moira said.

Barry was startled. She had never led. Always before she'd been second or third on a rope.

"I was thinking of rappelling down," he answered. "I can't see a clear route up."

"There," she said. "There and there and there." She jabbed her fingertip at a series of holds.

"But where would you set your protection?"

Her hand wove a series of stitches in the air. "There. Up there. To the side. Back across. Up about six feet."

His fear for her was not without reason. The climbing, after seeming so dangerous at first, had begun to lose its aura of hazard. They all fell from time to time, but their ropes kept them from suffering more than bruised knees and elbows. Then, one of the climbers who was leading had ignored instructions and, overconfident, had put in only one piece of protection. He placed it improperly, and when he slipped and fell, his weight jerked it loose. For a moment, no one had been able to move, then those who were not belaying or climbing had run toward the boy who lay sprawled on his back. Bright red blood seeped from his nose and ear.

"Jackets," Barry had demanded. Red Cross training that he'd not thought about in years came back with an intense clarity. "Every piece of clothing you can spare. We mustn't let him get cold."

They all had moved automatically, clumsily, unable to think. Having done as he instructed, they all stood stupefied. Their faces were shocked white beneath their tans.

He sent two of the students racing down the hill for help.

For an hour, they had huddled in a ragged circle around the

boy whose hair was paler than the sun-drenched grass and whose skin might have been molded from wax. He slipped in and out of consciousness. Each time his eyes shut, they all tensed, afraid that he had died. But then, he would groan or let out his breath harshly, and the moment would pass. Someone, Barry did not notice who, had started collecting gear. One, and then another, began to pack. They moved slowly, silently, as if any noise would disturb the delicate balance between life and death.

Grounded out. That was what they called it. Because his safety had not been properly set, he had grounded out. Barry remembered that the air force had been like that too. Pilots never failed. They never died. They bought it. *Grounded out.* The semantics covered up the fear.

Now, for a moment, it was as if, once again, he could hear the sharp, startled cry, see the backward arc, the body falling without grace or beauty, the rope writhing and twisting, the red-shirted boy settling in a cloud of unexpected dust.

"Ron," Barry protested, surprising himself at remembering the boy's name.

"Do you think I'd be so careless?"

It was asked in a tone that allowed no argument.

Stiffly, he stood up and tested his belay.

Don't climb, he thought, *it's too dangerous. Let us go back the way we came and find somewhere that'll always be safe.* But even as he thought it, he knew that it was impossible.

Once again, it was as if he were standing before the frizzy-haired girl, watching her long green nails sweep slowly before his face. At the time, he had not wanted to understand, "The world seeks balance," she'd said. "Extremism begets extremism."

"On belay," he said.

"Climbing," Moira replied.

His daughter, easily, with the supreme confidence of youth, grasped a handhold and pulled herself onto a flake. Smoothly, she worked her way up one side of the crack, straddled it and crossed over.

Below her, her father, ever watchful, full of fear, smoothly payed out the rope, determined to give her all the slack she needed, while at the same time keeping his hands tensed, ready to lock shut, ready to absorb the shock of any fall.

Wrinkles

===

"Albert?" Duke whispered. "Are you there?"

He'd delayed until five o'clock, until the sun had spread a thin band of pink along the crest of the Sooke Hills, until the forest beside him was fading and softening and the valley below was filling with shadow.

He waited beside the barbed wire fence. He was short and had long brown hair and wore an ankle-length coat the colour of drifted oak leaves. When there was no reply, he rose up on his toes, grasped the fence post and leaned forward, careful not to touch the rusted barbs. Although the failing sunlight lit the dirt road behind him, still filtered in dusty rays through the intermittent trees along the ditch, it did not penetrate the forest. It was late October and the rains had not yet begun in earnest, but only a few feet past where the forest began, the fallen leaves and lichen-covered deadfall were sodden. Here, yellow and black fungi clung to the tree trunks and ferns covered the ground.

"Albert?" he repeated, raising his voice slightly.

"Duke, that you?"

"You hophead. Where are you?" He grasped the fence post, fitted his boot to the lower strand and reached out with his other foot. He had come over the hill's crest, then down a quarter mile to this place. The unaccustomed exercise had made him sweat. The moment he entered the shadows, his skin felt clammy and he shivered.

What grew here, among the evergreens, was thin, the trunks drawn out like wires by their cruel struggle for sunlight. What should have been laurel and maple resembled pale vines with a

cluster of leaves. Duke found Albert sitting at the foot of an arbutus. He was wrapped in a grey wool blanket. Only his head and
his black runners showed.

Duke kicked away some dead branches, then sat down. "I
brought you a ham on rye. Large coffee with four sugars and two
creams."

"Gimme the coffee," Albert said.

"You ain't eaten for two days," he protested, but he knew there
was no point arguing. Sometimes Albert never ate for a week at a
time, living off endless cups of coffee heaped with sugar.

"You got smokes," Duke said.

"The Crow and the Puppet," Albert explained.

"They ain't got any money. It's a week to welfare. They're
dumpster diving."

"I panhandled some tourists."

They were sitting facing the valley. The field immediately before them was rugged, uncertain, a haphazard mixture of steep
rock, tree stumps, rotting logs and hollows. Beyond it, there was
another barbed wire fence, which surrounded a grove of Garry
oak and three black-and-white cows. An old bathtub used for
watering the stock sat near the gate. Here the ground fell away
more steeply and all they could see were the tops of a few trees,
but Duke could see the lay of the land in his mind's eye. It was
more open, grassy, and it flowed directly toward a cultivated field
and, finally, to a white, two-storey house. The house was set close
to the road, and in front of it there was a green wooden stand.
Duke had seen these stands in front of other places. There were
always flowers or vegetables (beets, zucchini, squash, carrots), a
sign saying "One dollar a bunch. Help yourself. Leave money in
can," and a metal can with a slot. He had no use for the vegetables, but once he had tried to take a can like that, only to find
that it was bolted to the wood. It had proved to him that country
people weren't as trusting as they let on and, therefore, deserved
no more consideration than city people.

The house sat in the centre of a yard that was surrounded by a
white picket fence, and even now, late in October, the gardens
were marked with splashes of orange and red from the late-
blooming chrysanthemums. From where they sat, they looked
down upon a patio with white and blue furniture. Off to one side

there was a wooden swing with seats so that people could sit opposite each other and be romantic.

"You weren't supposed to go near the harbour," Duke said.

"I can't sit and do nothing. I can't be cooped up. You know that. Besides, you're always saying to keep to my pattern. After a job, don't change your pattern. The street'll know it and then the cops'll know it."

"You've been down to the Kings."

"Nah, Duke."

"I know you. You get a couple of bucks and you go for a beer at the Kings."

"Just one," Albert protested.

"One. When did you stop at one?"

"That's all I could pay for. I pinched the Puppet's fags."

"Who'd you talk to?"

"Five minutes. I got two draft and sucked them up and I was gone."

They fell silent, stared at the white house. They knew the exterior by heart. Above ground basement. On the side they were facing, two basement windows. On the opposite side, downhill, two more windows. At the front, a verandah with two large windows and a light that was kept on all night. The first storey was high off the ground. The second storey was made up of a dormer with double windows. The roof was shallow. On its peak was an old TV antenna in the shape of a cross, but one arm had been broken and hung down. The antenna had come loose from its guy wires and leaned to one side.

Duke got up, walked away and hung one arm over an arbutus branch. The red line over the hills had changed to a pale green band. The sky above was a faint yellow, then pale blue. Above them, when he tipped his head back, he could see the sky had already turned black. "We agreed," he said. "No drinking until this is over."

"C'mon, Duke," Albert said, "don't be a shithead. I never talked to nobody. Give me a break. I can take care of myself."

"That's why you're eating off the Sally Ann."

"So are you."

"I didn't kill somebody." It was out. Duke hadn't meant to say it. They'd not talked about it directly since it had happened. It was as if by not mentioning it, they could undo it.

"I didn't tell nobody nothing. The Crow and I talked football. Blue Bombers and Roughriders. News. That's all."

"What kind of news?"

Duke kicked the tree. When things went wrong, he kicked things. Furniture, buildings, animals, people. Sometimes when he kicked things he yelled, but now he was silent. When the dull thud of his boot on wood quit, Albert said, "K.C.'s out on parole. Sharon's got a dose. They got a new dick at Eaton's. He's collaring everybody. He charged the Unit with lifting half a donut. He wouldn't even let him finish the second half. He said it was evidence."

Duke was studying the field, judging the distance, trying to fix in his mind where everything was. They didn't dare use flashlights. On the hillside, they could be seen for miles. He had been over it all before, even drawing himself maps on scraps of paper, then redoing them from memory. It would be different in the dark, though. He knew that. The dark changed everything. It made it safe but more complicated because there weren't as many landmarks to go by, the barbed wire fence on the far side of the field, the oak trees. It would get easier as they went down the hill, but here, at the beginning, it would be difficult, even dangerous. He would have preferred to walk down the road, but there were houses on the other side. People in the country noticed things, remembered things. They saw you twice and the second time said, you walked past here last week, I saw you when I was picking peas. Not much happened and so everything was an event.

"It's just the waiting," Albert said. "Not knowing what's going to happen next. I'm flopped somewhere and I'm wondering what are the cops doing now? What are they talking about? Who're they talking to? Then I gotta walk. You know how I gotta walk."

Duke turned back toward him, sat down so that their shoulders touched. "You got too much imagination. You shoulda been an artist." He took out the sandwich and began to eat it.

"The Raisin's in his box," Albert offered.

"The housekeeper gone?"

"She never stays overtime. Six o'clock and she's history."

"I brought you an Oh Henry."

Albert took the bar. "I come here at night to watch the Raisin and it gets dark and it's like I'm floating in space. All this stuff starts filling up my head. People yelling and stuff breaking and I feel like I'm ripping apart."

Jenny, Duke's girlfriend, alternated between home and the street. Two weeks before, Duke had got her to go home, get dressed in a skirt and blouse. She'd even put a ribbon in her hair and taken off her black lipstick. With white socks and blue runners, she'd looked like she was even younger than fourteen. She was used to giving the tourists sucker stories, so going up to the Raisin's front porch one evening, knocking and telling him some guy made her get out and walk, was easy. She'd even managed a few tears. The Raisin had invited her in, wanted to call the cops, wanted to call her parents. She'd talked him out of it, saying she didn't want to get into trouble, that she wasn't supposed to be in a car with boys. He'd made her hot chocolate and called her a cab. While she waited, she wandered from room to room, admiring his knickknacks. He collected dogs. Hundreds of them. All sizes.

"You dropped acid lately?" Duke asked.

Albert didn't bother to reply. It had been two months since he'd done any tabs. He had even quit magic mushrooms, walking away when there was a suitcase of them and he could have taken a handful. He hadn't done any pills until today either, but then the shaking had started and he'd bought a half-dozen Valium to get him through temporarily. They sat leaning against the tree and against each other, waiting, watching the house. Every night the routine had been the same. The living room light went off, the kitchen light went on, the kitchen light went off, a little later an upstairs light went on, then off, then another one on, then off, and the house was in darkness. At three o'clock the light went on when the Raisin went to the can. They planned to be long gone by three o'clock.

"Nothing's changed?" Duke asked. "He used to walk his dog."

"A white van came and took it away yesterday. It hasn't come back."

"The vet's. It has to have an operation. I heard him telling the checker at Shop Easy."

"I'd rather die than get so desperate I had to talk to checkers."

"The dog hasn't come back?"

"Nah. Two old ladies in flowerpot hats today. One of them wears white gloves. They had tea on the patio. He gave them some flowers from his garden. They came in a Caddy. Then a bald guy with a cane. He brought a bottle of booze and they drank it from teacups at the patio table."

"The housekeeper?" Duke asked.

"She hung out some carpets and beat hell out of them with a broom. I'd hate to be her kid."

"He can't have a housekeeper unless he's got money."

Albert shifted, scraped the leaves with one heel. "I don't like it, Duke. I don't think we should hit him."

"Are you crazy?" Duke snapped. "What've you been doing? Dropping by for tea every evening? He going to be your new uncle? Uncle Raisin."

The sudden conflict frightened them and they fell into silence. The only sound was the crunch of leaves and twigs as they shifted about. The kitchen light was on now. The ritual had begun. They both stared at the light, focussing on the golden rectangle, the sudden movement of the Raisin as he passed the window.

"I don't know," Albert sighed. "Wrinkle's boyfriend. Anybody else, okay."

"You've been converted. There was this voice said, 'Albert, give up your sinful ways.' I can see it now. Albert the Converted. You'll be preaching on the street corner with the Bible pushers. You'll be holding up these pamphlets. 'I was a bad boy and then God got me.' "

"I don't want to do it."

"Your mother got you to go to confession. You've told everything to Father Doohickey."

"Delany."

"Albert, we'll go in fast and get out fast. Two pillowcases full of bills."

"Louise Bennet." He pulled the blanket more tightly about him and put his head down on his knees.

"Who?" Duke hadn't been listening. He was already thinking about spending the money. Of buying airplane tickets out of Vancouver, of lying on the beach in Mexico. Of living in a hotel room, of eating when he wanted, sleeping when he wanted. No begging for handouts. No crawling to the dinner table and listening to his Old Man rant and rave when he couldn't stand being hungry any more.

"Wrinkles," Albert said. "That was her real name. Louise Bennet."

"I don't want to know about it. This is business. I told you that before. You got rabbits, don't give them names. Then you become friends with them, and when your old man kills them and your old lady fries them, you can't eat. And then your old man pounds you for being a sissy. You knock somebody on the head, you don't want to know their life story."

"She had two grandkids. She gave money to the Sally Ann every year."

"It was an accident. You didn't mean it."

"The paper says I hit her nine times. She had holes in her skull."

"There were extenuating circumstances. You were high. You just wanted to make her let go. You tried to run and she hung on.

"Man, she wouldn't let go," Albert burst out. "I tried. I said let go. Let go."

They had seen her around Cook Street village lots of times. An old lady in bright dresses and hats with flowers on them. She always carried a white purse. They'd never have paid attention to her if they hadn't been standing outside the bank on pension day and seen her boyfriend pointing at the wad of bills from her pension cheque. She had folded it over and put it in her purse. Her boyfriend shook his head in disapproval. They watched her cross the street and walk to her house. It was small, one storey, with a hedge all the way around it. She came out a few moments later, and she and the Raisin stood on the sidewalk, arguing, and he kept pointing his finger at the house and shaking his head. At last, he raised both hands in front of him, gave one last shake of his head, and then they went to the tearoom. Duke and Albert had been off B and Es since they'd turned eighteen, but it had got them thinking. The next pension day they hung around the laundromat, watching from the window, then Duke watched Wrinkles go to her house, and Albert followed her and the Raisin. They went to the tearoom. Then Wrinkles went to the Nearly New and rummaged through the racks. After that, she went to the bakery and bought bread and pastries. From the time she dropped off the money until she returned home took four hours.

It should have been easy. Instead, it was a screwup. The day they hit her place they waited until she was going in the tearoom door arm in arm with the Raisin. They jimmied a rear window and were taking the place apart when she appeared as if by magic. The Raisin had forgotten his hat, and she'd come back to get it for him. At least that's what the paper said. They never heard her until she screamed. Instead of fainting or running, she flung herself at Albert. He tried to get away but she hung on, screeching at the top of her lungs, and he took the hammer out of his pocket and hit her. Duke had been emptying a dresser in the bedroom. Albert was hitting her and would have still been whaling away when the cops arrived if Duke hadn't grabbed him by the arm and dragged him away. Then they were over a fence and down a back alley. They didn't stop until they got to the bushes in Beacon Hill. They lay there as the blood congealed on their clothes. When it got dark, they went to the pad where they'd stored their belongings in paper bags. They'd lived there once but didn't have a key any more, so they climbed onto the roof, dropped onto the patio and went in through the patio doors. Everybody was stoned or asleep. They showered and changed and took their blood-splattered clothes with them. The next day, they burned everything in an incinerator barrel. Albert put the hammer in a plastic bag and buried it.

"What," Albert said, "am I going to tell the judge? I hit her nine times by accident?" His face was sideways on his knees. A last flash of sunlight suddenly illuminated his face. For a moment, he might have been mistaken for a lost child.

"We've gotta have money for airplane tickets, motels, food, clothes. You gonna borrow it from the bank?" Duke picked up a branch and went to lean on it. It broke in half. The wood here looked solid but was weak with dry rot. It broke under the slightest pressure. "Sergeant Stevens dropped by your mom's place today. She came looking for me. She wanted to know were you in trouble again."

"He's narcotics."

"He got promoted."

"Why didn't she let go?" The cops are always telling them, don't be a hero."

"We've got to do it, Albert. You hated school because they

made you sit still, you had to be out walking. If you don't walk, you go crazy. You hated bells. In prison there's bells for everything. You hated being given orders. Tell that to the screws."

"I don't think he's got any money."

"No money?"

"No."

"He asks me to carry his groceries. He tips me two bucks. Two bucks," Duke said, repeating the wonder of it, "and drops his wallet and it's got so many fifties he can barely close it."

"You shoulda grabbed it. We'd be gone now."

"He told the Six Four Nine chick that he doesn't believe in banks. Man, I'm telling you. He goes to Shop Easy, he pays cash. He goes to the bakery, he pays cash. The tearoom, cash. No credit cards. I'm following along behind him carrying all this stuff he's buying, and he's telling me he doesn't believe in credit cards. Where's his money? At home. Under the carpet, in the freezer, in the sugar canister. You've read about people like that. They eat cat food, and when they die, the cops find a million bucks stashed around the house."

"I seen the Freak Broad down at the harbour," Albert said. His voice was soft, vague, as if he were far away. He fell into moods like this, but it was usually when he was reading comic books. He loved comic books. When he had money, he bought them by the armload and carried them around in shopping bags. Once he started reading them, there was no use trying to talk sense to him. He'd order coffee at Denny's and sit and read until they kicked him out. Then he'd go somewhere else and order another coffee. "No tricks since the weather got cold. She read her cards. She says it's a bad time to take risks."

"Time for her to go south. Time for us to go south."

Albert pulled himself more tightly into the blanket, making himself smaller, then burst out. "It'll be like the bag lady. You said she had all the dough stashed in her shopping cart. She doesn't spend it on nothing, you said. It has to be there, right? She gets her welfare cheques. She don't pay rent. She sleeps in the park. She eats off the Mustard Seed. Let's track her, you said. Nothing better to do, right. Two days. Up and down Fort. Up and down Beacon Hill. Yessirree, you said. Loaded. You knock her down, Albert, and I'll grab her shopping cart. Yessirree, big hit. Scarface Al and the Duke. Running down the street pushing a grocery cart and this fat broad screaming after us. And what'd we get?"

Duke didn't say anything. Once Albert started, there was no stopping him. Duke had learned to wait until he ran down. When he did, when he got it all out, he became reasonable again.

"Brassieres. A shopping bag of brassieres. All sizes. The crime of the century. And a bag of panties. A bag of sweaters."

"Crime Stoppers is offering two thousand bucks," Duke snapped. He hadn't meant to get annoyed. He'd made up his mind to control his temper. "The Freak Broad would turn you in for fifty."

"I can't do it, that's all."

"Okay."

"I can't."

"Fine."

"You're always pushing me, pushing me. In grade six it was let's boost chains from K-Mart."

"We did okay."

"In grade eight, let's start dealing."

"You done good. You didn't say you didn't want the money. You bought a ghetto blaster, you bought posters. You treated the chicks."

"We ended up in juvie."

"You're going to end up in a cage until you're forty-five." Duke's voice was harsh, impatient. "There's nothing worse than that. Your social worker can't talk the judge into community service for this one. They don't care you haven't got a daddy. They don't care you got a reading problem. You've used those up. Superman isn't going to drop out of the sky and make things better."

"We got other choices."

"Sure. We run behind a Brink's truck and hope a bag of money falls off."

"The Chink store across the school. You go in and make noise by the freezer. I'll grab what's in the till."

"I tried to break a fifty there. So solly, no change big dolla. Besides, her old man's in the back with a meat cleaver. You put your claws in his till and he chops them off."

"We can get it off the street."

"That's just the poor stealing off the poor," Duke said.

"Punky's dealing coke."

"You trying to commit suicide?"

"What about Joe Army? He's got an operation."

"Sure."

"Hydroponics," Albert said.

"Hydrobullshit."

"I heard it at the Kings. It means growing without soil. Like tomatoes and cucumbers."

"He's growing tomatoes?"

"Homegrown. In his attic. Big heat lamps. Quality stuff. Lots of tubing. Looks like chemistry class. He keeps his stash in a black garbage bag."

"You got a gun?" Duke asked. "You been inside? You know who else is there? You know who his muscle is?"

"I gotta walk. I can't think sitting down."

"How many times have you called me in the middle of the night and said, 'Duke, I gotta walk,' and I walked with you? We walked to Sidney. We walked to Sooke. We walked all night. When your old man blew his head off, we walked for two days."

"Nobody forced you," Albert said resentfully. He didn't like to be reminded of those times. Walking all night. Stopping periodically at donut shops, walking with nowhere to go. When it was over, when he couldn't walk any more and they took a bus or hitchhiked back, he always felt cheated. He felt that, somewhere, if he could remember where, there was a place for him, a shack on the beach maybe, or a converted garage, a place with a stove and a bed and a table and a chair, a place when he saw it, he would know was his.

"I had to steal new shoes because of you," Duke said.

Albert laughed abruptly. The laughter was short, choppy, nearly hysterical. He began to rock back and forth. "Grimsdale would love this. You and me in deep shit and fighting. The day he kicked me out of school, he said, 'Albert, my boy, if you don't change your ways, you'll come to a bad end.' "

"Grimsdale," Duke said, remembering. Grimsdale had always

pounded down the paper in his wastebasket by stepping on it. They'd filled the wastebasket with water. They'd glued the drawers of his desk shut.

"Remember what he used to quote? Something, something, something, and masters of our fate."

"Can it."

"That's what I told Grimsdale," Albert said.

They both laughed, but this time it was easier, more familiar. They had a Grimsdale routine. Neither of them had seen him for six years, but they remembered his every move, demonstrating for their friends the short, tight strut, the quick jerk of his chin. They could repeat every word he'd ever said to them.

"My boy," Duke said, "this hurts me more than it hurts you..."

"But for the good of the academic community..." Albert added, picking up the familiar line.

"You must go."

"My boy, you have talent..." Albert started.

"You have intelligence..."

"You can be..."

"Anything you want," Duke ended.

They both laughed, pushed each other with their shoulders, then realizing they had been noisy, stopped, waited, then laughed more quietly.

"There goes the kitchen light," Duke said. "By the time we get there, he'll be asleep."

They waited for another moment. There was the rasp of their clothes, their own breathing, the subtle crackle of rotting leaves and wood, then a dog began to bark somewhere close by. Duke sat up straight.

"How come," Albert said, "you're afraid of dogs?"

"I'm not afraid. I just don't like them."

"You wouldn't go through with that B and E in Oak Bay because they had a wiener dog in the house."

Duke didn't reply but got up, shook himself and brushed at the dirt that clung to his coat. The light had long faded. Overhead, the moon was rising, full and pale. Stars were out. Below them, the bathtub gleamed like a shrine. Here and there, rectangles of light marked the drowned houses.

They followed the light below them like a beacon. The land fell sharply, and in places they had to cling to vegetation, feeling their way down, avoiding tangles of spine-covered bramble, sudden sharp rock faces, fallen tree trunks. They tripped and fell on the rough ground, thin stems whipped their faces, burning nettle stung their hands. If Duke or Albert had been alone, either one would have given up, turned back, but they encouraged each other, hissing or whistling as one or the other found a clear path. The moonlight, although it was pale, lit their way. At the barbed wire fence, Duke ripped his hand, but he was used to pain. He wiped the blood away on his pants. They nervously skirted the unfamiliar cows. Here, the oak leaves rattled like dry bones. At last they came out on a long easy slope covered with mown grass and ran the last distance, letting the weight of their bodies drag them toward the lit window.

Just as they reached the picket fence, there was a snort and the sudden clatter of hooves on stone. They both dropped to the ground.

"What was that?" Duke asked.

"I don't know," Albert whispered. "I hate the country. There's all these noises. In the city I know what they are. I'm in an alley and I hear something and I know that's a cat, that's a drunk, that's guys shooting up. I can tell a cop by the sound of his feet. Out here, I don't know what anything is."

"The country is where you get your food from."

"I get my food from 7-Eleven."

Duke stood up. The patio furniture glowed silver in the moonlight. A white fountain rose like a petrified flower. Up close, the house looked larger, more formidable.

"You tell Jenny about tonight?" Albert asked.

"Not a chance. You tell a chick things, you can't ever leave them. They're into revenge. You tell Susy?"

"We're not that close."

They jumped over the fence. Duke stopped before a fish pond. He pointed toward the swing. "Do you think this is where he brought Wrinkles? You think they used to come out here and do it?"

"Too old."

"You know," Duke said quietly, "wrinkle to wrinkle. The two

raisins. Imagine if their wrinkles got stuck together and they couldn't pull loose."

They knelt at a basement window and Duke pressed strips of tape over the glass. He took a lead weight out of his pocket. It was wrapped in a wool sock. He hit the glass sharply. There was a sudden breaking. Carefully, he pulled the glass loose, then picked pieces out of the frame. He reached inside for the latch. He stopped, felt, then felt again, running his hand over chain link, testing it, pushing and pulling. Finally, he leaned his weight against it. When it wouldn't budge, he pulled his hand back. Albert reached in, touched it and sat back.

"That's that then," Albert said.

"What's what?" Duke asked.

"Have you got wire cutters? I haven't."

"Fort Knox," Duke said.

"You're crazy. You've got a one-track mind."

"Think about it," Duke whispered fiercely. "Nobody wires their windows without a reason."

"Forget it. Let's go to the Kings."

"Grimsdale."

"Forget Grimsdale."

"Remember what he taught us about Hong Kong? The Brits blocked the front but not the back."

"This isn't Hong Kong."

"Everybody misses something. Something staring them in the face. They get focussed and miss it."

Duke went to the back, braved the light, but the door frame overlapped the edge. There was no way to get his screwdriver into the crack so he could pop open the lock. The small window was too high to let him reach the inside handle. Albert followed him as he went along the other side. The two windows also were covered with mesh and the first floor windows were beyond reach. He quickly looked about the side yard, but there was no ladder, nothing he could stand on to reach the sills.

They scurried past the verandah and its revealing pool of light. They had nearly completed their circle. The moon was once more behind them.

"What's this?" Duke said. He caught hold of a metal handle and pulled. An iron cover lifted up with the snarl of rusted metal.

He reached inside, felt the sharp slope down, the metal bed. He felt the sides. They were of tin.

"Bazoom," he said. "A coal chute. Grimsdale, you were a genius."

"Duke. . ."

Duke cut him off. "Bucks, Albert. We don't have to worry no more. No more twenty-five years in the pokey. No more monkey in a cage."

"I'm not going in there."

"You chickenshit."

"Duke, come on, let's forget it. You and me. We'll hitchhike to T.O."

"Listen," Duke grabbed him by his shirt, "every time you think you can't do this, you just imagine being put in a cage until you're forty-five. And you make a noise, they put you in solitary. No windows. In the hole. There's nothing worse than that."

Duke pulled off his coat, kneeled down with his back to the wall and put one leg into the chute. "I'll drop down, and when I get in I'll open the back door." He put his weight on his hands and put his other leg into the chute. As he wiggled backwards, the metal studs on his jeans scraped on the metal. When he was in up to his shoulders, with his elbows hooked over the edge, he stopped and said, "This is two you owe me." Then he wiggled in farther, grabbing the edge with first one hand, then the other. The chute now ended at his hips. He tried to reach back with his right foot but couldn't feel anything so he let his arms straighten out. As he did so, his hips slipped over the edge. With his arms fully extended, he could bend the lower part of his body flat with the wall. He tried to get a purchase but the toes of his boots slipped on the concrete.

"Take my right hand," he said. And when Albert did, he let go with the left, inched down and tried to touch the floor. Instead, the splash of water echoed hollowly. Instinctively, he pulled up his foot, tried to find a purchase. The chute's edge was just beyond the reach of his left hand.

"Get me out of here."

"Duke," Albert said.

"Come on," Duke said, his voice tight with fear. "There's water down there. Pull me out."

"Let him go," the Raisin said. He had crept up beside Albert.

"Who's there?" Duke said. "Who's that?"

"That him?" the Raisin said. "He killed my Louise?"

"I can't," Albert said, "I can't do it." But the Raisin slammed down the iron cover on his arms and he let go.

"That him?" the Raisin said. He had the hammer in his hand. "You're sure that's him?"

Duke's voice echoed faintly from the chute, rose in fragments of sound.

"Here's your money," the Raisin said.

"Let him out," Albert shouted. "I can't do this. It's not worth it."

"Take it. Go away. Don't come back for a long time. After I'm gone." The Raisin stuffed the envelope into Albert's pocket.

"He's a good swimmer. Get a rope. We'll pull him out."

"It's a cistern. Straight concrete walls. He's not getting out."

"Duke," Albert yelled and pulled at the iron cover, but the Raisin slammed it with the hammer. Albert put his hands to his head and jerked back and forth. He raised his hands and put them down. "Duke," he yelled again, but it did no good. He shook his head as if to free it from the Valium, then said, "I've got to walk," as if he were talking to no one at all and turned and stumbled into the darkness.

"We were going to be married," the Raisin yelled after him. "She was going to be my bride."

Identities

≡

Normally, he goes clean-shaven into the world, but the promise of a Saturday liquid with sunshine draws him first from his study to the back yard, from there to his front lawn. The smell of burning leaves stirs the memories of childhood car rides, narrow lanes adrift with yellow leaves, girls on plodding horses, unattended stands piled high with pumpkins, onions, beets, so that each one was, in its own way, a still life. Always, there were salmon tins glinting with silver, set above hand-painted signs instructing purchasers to deposit twenty-five or fifty cents. This act of faith, containing all the stories he has read in childhood about the North—cabins left unlocked, filled with supplies for hapless wayfarers—wakes in him a desire to temporarily abandon the twice-cut yards and hundred-year-old oaks.

He does not hurry, for he has no destination. He meanders, instead, through the suburban labyrinth of cul-de-sacs, bays and circles, losing and finding himself endlessly. Becoming lost is made all the easier because the houses repeat themselves with superficial variations. There grows within him, however, a vague unease with symmetry, with nothing left to chance, no ragged edges, no unkempt vacant lots, no houses rendered unique by necessity and indifference.

The houses all face the sun. They have no artificial divisions. There is room enough for everyone. Now, as he passes grey stone gates, the yards are all proscribed by stiff picket fences, and quickly, a certain untidiness creeps in: a fragment of glass, a chocolate bar wrapper, a plastic horse, cracked sidewalks with ridges of stiff grass. Although he has on blue jeans—matching pants and jacket made in Paris—he is driving a grey Mercedes Benz. Gangs of young men follow the car with their unblinking eyes. The young men stand and lean in tired, watchful knots close to phone booths and seedy-looking grocery stores.

Their hair glistens as though shellacked. Their jackets gleam with studs. Eagles, tigers, wolves and serpents ride their backs.

He passes a ten-foot wire fence enclosing a playground bare of equipment and pounded flat. The gate is double locked, the fence cut and rolled into a cone. Three boys throw stones at pigeons. Paper clogs the fence like drifted snow. The school is sheathed in heavy screens. Its yellow brick is pockmarked, chipped.

The houses are squat, as though they were once taller and have, slowly, sunk into the ground. Each has a band of dirt around the bottom. The blue glow of television sets lights the windows. On the front steps of a red-roofed house, a man sits. He wears black pants, a tartan vest, a brown snap-brimmed hat. Beside him is a suitcase.

Fences here are little more than fragments. Cars jam the narrow streets, and he worries that he might strike the unkempt children who dart back and forth like startled fish. Street lights come on. He takes them as a signal to return the way he came, but it has been a reckless, haphazard path. Retracing it is impossible. He is overtaken by sudden guilt. He has left no message for his wife.

There have been no trees or drifting leaves, no stands covered in produce, no salmon tins, but time has run away with him. His wife, he realizes, will have returned from bridge, his children gathered for supper. He also knows that, at first, they have blamed his absence on a neighbour's hospitality and gin. However, by the time he can return, annoyance will have blossomed into alarm. His safe return will, he knows from childhood and years of being locked in domestic grief, degenerate to recriminations and apology.

Faced with this, he decides to call the next time he sees a store or phone booth. So intent is he upon the future that he dangerously ignores the present and does not notice the police car, concealed in the shadows of a side street, nose out and follow him.

Ahead, there is a small store with windows covered in hand-painted signs and vertical metal bars. On the edge of the light, three young men and a girl slouch. One of the men has a beard, and in spite of the advancing darkness, wears sunglasses. He has on a fringed leather vest. His companions wear leather jackets. Their peaked caps make their heads seem flat, their foreheads nonexistent. The girl is better looking than she should be for such companions. She is long-legged and wears a white turtleneck sweater that accentuates her breasts.

In spite of his car, he hopes his day-old beard, which he strokes upward with the heel of his hand, will, when combined with his clothes, provide immunity. He slips his wallet into his shirt pocket, does up the metal buttons on his jacket and slips a ten-dollar bill into his back pocket. Recalling a television show, he decides that if he is accosted, he will say that the ten is all he's got, that he stole the car and ask them if they know a buyer.

He eases out of the car, edges nervously along the fender and past the grille. The store window illuminates the sidewalk like a stage. Beyond the light, everything is obscured by darkness. He is so intent upon the three men and the girl that he does not notice the police car drift against the curb, nor the officer who advances with a pistol in his hand.

When the officer, who is inexperienced, who is nervous because of the neighbourhood, who is suspicious because of the car and because he has been trained to see an unshaven man in blue jeans as a potential thief and not as a probable owner, orders him to halt, he is surprised. When he turns part way around and recognizes the uniform, he does not feel fear but relief. Instinctively relaxing, certain of his safety, in the last voluntary movement of his life, he reaches his hand toward his wallet for his identity.

Seiche

They had partied most of the night, fallen asleep in Sammy's car. They wakened in darkness and staggered into the false dawn. They bagged a mallard and two teal before the birds left to feed in the grain fields, and then with nothing to do but watch for strays and wait until the ducks returned, they pulled their boat onto a small island, had one beer, then another and another. The dawn had been chilly, but as the sun rose the wind dropped and the day turned warm. They fell asleep on the dry reeds, three hunters in waders and parkas lying around a single dead willow like dark spokes in a broken wheel.

"Jim, the boat's gone."

"What do you mean, it's gone? It can't be gone!"

"Sammy?"

"What the hell, Sammy. Is this one of your practical jokes?"

"Sure," Sammy says, but he isn't paying attention to them. Instead, he is turning slowly in a circle, hand cupped over his eyes, searching the reed beds.

"Joke's over, Sammy," Bob says. "I want a beer and a sandwich. Tell your friend to bring back the boat before I break your scrawny neck."

"Nobody took the boat," Sammy says.

Bob cups his hands to this mouth and yells, "Hey, whoever you are. Come in out of the reeds. Joke's over. Bring back the boat." He turns to Jim and winks. "Shit, can you imagine really being stuck in the middle of a swamp? Sammy, you're nuts. This is worse than when you stopped the elevator for an hour."

"I woke up and the boat was gone."

"Here it comes, Jim. The boat story."

"If we're going to get any hunting in, we need to get started. The sun's going down. I don't want to be wandering around these channels in the dark," Jim says.

"It was gone, okay?"

"Sure, Sammy," Bob says. "Somebody stole it. We're in the middle of the bloody marsh and somebody just came up and said here's a boat and these guys don't look like they're using it."

Bob is large, heavyset, an ex-football player. Until his knee was wrecked during a practice, he played for the Roughriders. Now, he's overweight and has a noticeable limp.

Jim is short, has a blond crew cut, holds himself stiffly. Even after six beers, he is wary, his eyes watching everything. "You're the expert, Sambo," Jim says.

"Jim, it's a joke," Bob says. "I can hear him telling everybody in the office. Boy, did I get those suckers. Remember the time he was going to take us to the bootlegger's? Lost, he said, and led us around the bloody bush for hours."

"The boat was tied up, Sambo," Jim says. He's never taken his eyes off Sammy's face, watching for any telltale twitch at the corner of his mouth.

"Was it?" Sammy asks.

"Was it what?"

"Tied up."

"Bob tied it up."

"Did he?"

"Did you, Bob?"

"Sure," Bob says.

"Sure what?" Sammy asks. He's turned in a slow circle, bending his head, searching the reed beds, the winding grey channels.

"Sure I tied it up."

"There are no waves," Jim says.

"The wind's from the northeast," Sammy says.

"What's that supposed to mean?"

"A seiche," Sammy says. "I've heard about it but I've never seen it before. If the wind blows from the northeast, it pushes water southwest into the marshes."

They all study the tops of the reeds. The marsh is like an endless field of grain. As they watch, the tops of the bullrushes bend toward the southwest, lift, then bend down again.

"How much higher is the water going to get?" Bob asks.

"Not much higher," Sammy replies, but for the first time he notices the marsh grass hanging in the crooks of the branches.

He lived in this area for two years when he was in high school, cut classes to hunt geese. His family had moved every year but this was to be the last move. For the first time, they bought a house. When his father died unexpectedly, his mother moved them to Winnipeg, a city where Sammy has since accumulated two ex-wives, five ex-jobs and two ex-houses, and now sublets a condominium with white walls, white furniture and a single fern hanging from the ceiling. He returns frequently. Gradually, his friends from high school have drifted away, but he sits in the parlour, waiting for the appearance of vaguely familiar faces, buys rounds of beer, invites his former classmates to visit him in the city. Each time, he makes a tour of the town, getting his hair cut, mailing a letter in the post office, buying some small item in the butcher shop. He drives past the high school, the house (now painted grey), the beach, the dock (where, during the summer nights, he tested his nerve by diving to the bottom of the lake to raise up heavy granite stones), the movie house, the place where the Chinese restaurant used to be. Every fall, he and Bob and Jim come for a long weekend to hunt ducks.

"I shouldn't have come," Bob says. "Lorraine said I shouldn't. She said, 'What are you going there for? You don't even like ducks. I cook it and you won't eat it.'"

"Did you tell her where we were going?" Sammy asks, his voice quiet, controlled, as if the answer is unimportant.

"Sure, I told her," Bob starts, but then he stops, his voice trails away. "Well, I said, you know." He shrugs. "We're going hunting in the marsh."

"There are a lot of marshes," Jim says.

"Jim?" Sammy asks.

"I left a note on the kitchen table for Mrs. Melvin, but she won't read it until tomorrow morning. What about you? You're always saying how you're visiting local friends."

"Things have changed," Sammy says. "You guys know that. People get married. They move away."

"You're always driving down here."

"I stay at the motel mostly. Go to the parlour for a few beers."

Jim notices Sammy studying the willow. The stem is as thick as a fist, the bark corrugated and scarred. Most of the branches have broken off. The few at the top are wound with marsh grass.

"What are you guys looking at?" Bob says.

"We'll be fine," Sammy says. "You're right. This place is like Portage and Main. Someone will see us."

"You got that look," Bob says, "the way you get during sales meetings when something's up."

As if to confirm what Sammy has said, there are three shots just west of them. Sammy replies with three shots.

"They can't see us," Jim says. "We need a pole or something."

Jim starts to wrestle with the dead willow, rocking it back and forth, trying to wrench the tangled roots loose.

"Don't," Sammy says. "If the water gets higher, we may need something to hang onto. The roots are all that hold this stuff together." He jumps up and down and they can feel the ground quiver.

Sammy puts his red cap on the end of his shotgun. He waves it back and forth but it gets no response.

"Are you guys going to tell me or what?" Bob says. He's been looking at one, then the other.

Sammy points at the marsh grass. Bob is puzzled but realizes they are both serious. He cups his hand as if to hold any answer they will offer him. Both of them look away, search the marsh, try to pick out movement in the growing shadows.

"You're crazy," Bob says all at once. "How could the water get that high?" He holds his hand, palm down, at the level of the marsh grass. It comes to his shoulders. "We're not going to end up standing in five feet of water. That's nuts. Nobody could do that. Standing all night. It's September."

"How long does something like this last?" Jim asks.

"As long as the wind blows, I guess." They have both turned to look east toward the shallow water, the rising ground, the highway that runs along the marsh's edge.

"Nobody could do it," Bob protests. "I'm telling you. Do you think you could do it, Jim? Sammy? I'm telling you, we used to play our games in the rain and we were so numb we couldn't feel anything. We had to have help getting our uniforms off."

"There!" Sammy says.

"What?"

"Something."

"I don't see anything," Jim says.

"Something flashed."

"Damn these reeds," Bob says.

"Are you sure?"

"I don't know. I wasn't looking straight at it. I just saw this flash out of the corner of my eye."

"Sun on the water," Jim says.

"If we just had something to stand on," Bob says.

"I could get up on your shoulders," Jim offers. He's the shortest, lightest.

"There!" Sammy says.

"Where?"

The shadows are gathering, pooling in the reed beds, stretching over the water.

"I saw it, too," Bob agrees.

"A canoe," Sammy says, his voice full of relief.

To the east, there is the dark outline of a boat and two men. Bob and Jim begin to fire while Sammy waves his cap. Between them they fire thirty shots. The boat never changes its path and disappears to the south in a patch of reeds. They begin to yell and Sammy whistles shrilly through his teeth. When they stop, there is nothing but water and reeds and sky and silence and Bob says, "We're going to die."

"Nobody is going to die," Sammy says.

"We're going to drown," Bob says.

"Nobody is going to drown," Sammy says. "There are lots of boats. Somebody will see us."

Ducks and geese are returning from the grain fields. The birds skim the reeds, land all around the three men. There is a steady firing by hunters, now close, now farther away. Hunters in boats, hunters on the marsh edge, hunters on the sandspit that separates the marsh from the lake.

"Lorraine is going to be really pissed off," Bob says. "I was supposed to be home by ten so that we could go over the wedding invitations."

"To hell with Lorraine," Sammy shouts.

"At least she hasn't given me the clap. That's more than you can say for what's-her-name with the white cowboy boots."

"I don't introduce myself to every prospect by saying, 'I'm Big Bob, you must have seen me play with the Roughriders.' "

"That's because a skinny little runt like you couldn't even be a waterboy."

"Lorraine, Lorraine, Lorraine, that's all you talk about."

"And all you talk about is this town. All it's got is one main street, three stores and a beer parlour. You'd think it was Toronto, the way you talk." They are both yelling, their voices sharp pitched. Bob rolls his shoulders in imitation of Sammy. "Well, I went home this weekend. Had a great time. Got invited out for supper. Stayed over with my friends."

"Shut up," Jim says.

"We'll be fine," Sammy shouts. He wants to stop but he can't. "I've been in tighter spots than this. I ran away from home and I was hitchhiking and two guys picked me up and they were drunk out of their minds and they were driving a hundred miles an hour and we missed a turn and that car went end over end and I got blown right out the rear window. I had a guy in Alberta pull a gun on me and say he was going to feed me to his dogs and he would have except his gun jammed and I ran right over him getting out of there. I always did what I wanted until I took this job and when we get back to town the first thing I'm doing I'm quitting and I'm going to do what I want with my life. We'll be fine."

After Sammy's outburst, they all stand silent. While they've been arguing, the water has covered the island, risen up past their ankles. The tops of the bullrushes flatten, press farther down.

"We've got to think of something positive," Jim says.

"Sure, Captain Marvel. Close your eyes and imagine a boat coming to get us."

"You've got a bad attitude, Sammy."

Sammy laughs out loud, throws his arms in the air. "We're going to be up to our necks in freezing water in an hour and I've got a bad attitude. You sound like my old man. Keep a stiff upper lip, boy, he used to say. He couldn't even keep a job more than two years in a row, but he wanted me to keep a stiff upper lip. Things will be better by and by."

It is the first time in the six years they have known him that Sammy has mentioned his family. Bob and Jim say nothing, look off into the growing darkness, at the blood-red line of the sunset. When they move, their feet make sucking sounds. The reed and silt island is softening, disintegrating beneath them.

"We need a torch," Bob says at last.

"I'll order one from the store," Sammy says.

"No. From the bullrushes."

They tear off three dry bullrush stems, pull the heads loose, attempt to light them with matches, but the seeds flash and die. They take paper from their pockets, two pieces of kleenex, a grocery list, then rifle their wallets, tearing holes in the centre of the bills, force them over a bullrush head so that the bills are like a series of wings.

"Shit!" Bob says, looking at the money. Some of the bills are twenties.

Jim strikes a match, cups it against his body, holds it to the paper, which catches, goes out, then catches again. Bob raises the bills high over his head. The other two take their shotguns from where they have set them in the branches of the willow and begin to shoot. The torch burns with a wavering, shaking flame, and the shotguns, each time they are fired, give bursts of light. The bills burn loose, pieces spin into the darkness, land on the water and go out. When the last piece of paper has fallen, Bob throws the torch away. They wait, straining to hear if anyone is calling to them. In the darkness, there is only the dry sound of reeds rasping against each other and the creak and rub of their clothes.

The water is rising faster, reaches up their thighs. The dark is thick, impenetrable. The moon rises round and full and drives a golden dagger toward and through them.

"Somebody's going to have to swim," Jim says.

"Don't be crazy," Bob replies. "You'll just get tangled in the reeds. You couldn't swim in here even in daylight. At least you're still alive and as long as you're alive, there's a chance."

"Think about McPherson's office," Sammy says. "You said you were going to get it. You try swimming and you'll never get it."

"That's right," Bob says. "And what about your house? You said you were going to repaint it and fix the roof. Man, you love that house. You don't want someone else living in it."

They wait for a sign that someone has noticed their torch, but there is nothing. In the darkness they edge closer to the willow tree, touch it for comfort. There is no sound as the water rises, no sensation of current, just a steady upward pressure, an enclosing coldness. They stand with their backs to each other, looking outward. When the water begins to trickle over his chest waders, Jim gasps, breathes between clenched teeth. He is the shortest, and the other two, listening to him groan and shift about, feel the water move upward on their own waders, pray that the wind will stop before the water begins to trickle and then run in below their armpits.

"Jim," Bob says.

"Hey, Jim," Sammy says.

Jim doesn't reply. He is shaking with cold, has his teeth clenched to stop their chattering.

"Hey, Pink Cadillac Jim. Nobody defeats Pink Cadillac Jim."

"Go to hell!" Jim manages to grunt out the words without unclenching his teeth. Normally, only when they're all drunk do they dare talk this way to him. When he was twenty and a delivery boy in the mail room, he bought a pink Cadillac convertible and parked it beside the president's parking space. Except for the intervention of a great-uncle who worked in the company, he would have been fired. Instead, he was given a lecture on company politics and told to take the bus to work. Three months later, because he couldn't keep up the payments, he lost the Caddy, but the story, even after ten years, still makes the rounds at office parties.

Fifteen minutes more, and the water begins to seep into Sammy's waders, soaking his clothes, encasing him in numbness. Finally, the water rises to Jim's chin and, miraculously, stops. In the darkness, their heads rest on the surface like severed heads of criminals or martyrs. The willow tree is completely submerged. The grass caught in the branches trails out like the hair of a drowned woman.

Sammy holds his shotgun over his shoulder. His cap is on it. If anyone comes close, he hopes to lift up the shotgun and wave the cap to get their attention. The water being driven into the marsh

by the northeast wind pushes against him, and he has to hold
tight to the tree so that he does not float away. His feet lift in the
water, and he has to force them back down, dig in his heels. The
silence fills all the spaces, fills up their ears and eyes and mouths,
fills up their heads. It is like they are asleep.

"Sammy," Jim says.

"Yeah."

"Recite the alphabet."

"What?"

"Sammy."

"Yeah."

"What's your name?"

"Samuel Delenore Thompson."

"Delenore?"

"What?"

"You said Delenore. What the hell is Delenore?"

"Mother's maiden name."

"You were asleep."

"No."

"Yeah."

"Bob there?"

"Yeah."

"The water in your waders yet?"

"An hour ago. I told you when it happened."

"What time is it?"

"I don't know," Bob says. "My watch quit."

"Cheap bloody watch," Sammy says.

They are too cold to laugh, but for a moment, they are together
again, the three of them outside a bar, an alky banging at the car
window, offering them a Longines watch, and they're saying no,
no, they don't need watches and they drive into the traffic, but
when they are stopped at a red light and the alky runs up, bangs
on the window again, Bob, thinking the watch must be stolen,
pulls twenty-five dollars out of his pocket and shoves it through
the partly open window and the alky drops the watch and says
he's got more and Jim and Sammy, not wanting to miss out on a
good deal, rip out twenty-five dollars each and then the alky's
gone, unable to believe his good fortune, racing for the nearest

beer parlour, and it isn't until they're five blocks away that one of them notices the name on the watch is Long-Green and after swearing and shouting, they laugh all the way home, and ever since, when one of them asks the other for the time, no one knows why they burst out laughing.

"Sammy," Bob says.

"Yeah."

"This town you love so much. It's a hole. It's got a parlour, three stores and a barbershop."

"Don't knock my town."

"It's not even a town. There's more dogs than people."

"And you can't tell the difference," Jim adds.

"It's all I've got," Sammy says.

"Sammy?" Bob says.

"Yeah."

"You going to be my best man?"

"Me?"

"Sure."

"Lorraine'll have a fit." He hasn't been a favourite with Lorraine since last July when he put a fish under the dashboard of Bob's car. It took Bob three days to figure out where the smell was coming from.

"She says no jokes. Promise!"

"Yeah."

The cold makes them cough, short catching coughs in the front of their chests. Sammy is very thin, and the cold works its way through him until he is coughing most of the time. When he coughs, he can't bend forward to ease the pain in his chest because then his face is in the water. Later, but none of them know how much later, there is just darkness and cold and fear, and Jim says, "I thought I saw a light."

"Did you see anything, Sammy?" Bob asks.

"Nothing, Quarterback."

"Don't call me Quarterback."

"What are you going to do? Drown me?"

"When we get out of here, I'll wring your neck."

"Hup, hup, thirteen, twenty," Sammy says, but the effort starts him coughing again.

"You can't even get it right. You count first," Bob says, "then you say hup."

"I should never have asked you guys to come," Sammy says.

"Don't get sentimental on me," Bob answers. "Just give me the Brownlee account."

"Yeah, I'll take the Jacobs," Jim says. Because he's shortest, he's having the hardest time keeping the water away from his face. For the last two hours, he's been redecorating his house, getting everything exactly as he'd like it, organizing the details of the yard.

"You were right. I was the expert," Sammy says.

"Is this the guy who calls me the Gimp when he gets mad?" Bob says. If he could, he'd yell and stamp around, give a performance that would fill up the marsh. At work, his ranting terrifies secretaries, but Sammy and Jim just ignore it.

"I never called you the Gimp."

"Sure you did. After I got the big order for the Carlton. I heard you raving in the washroom. Goddamn Gimp, you were yelling. I thought you were going to rip out the sink."

"I worked on that order."

"You've got to learn to know a fake pass when you see one."

"Life isn't football."

"No," Bob agrees, "but it will do."

They try to keep talking, keep reassuring each other that they are still alive. When they cannot get an answer to a question, they goad each other, drive their voices through the darkness that has entered their heads and is smothering them.

"I told Lorraine, when we get married, she's quitting," Bob says. "I've had enough of eating out of cans and coming home to an empty apartment. Besides, mine's mine. No more Sammy watching her when she's bending over the filing cabinet. Right, Sammy?"

"Yeah," Sammy says, but his voice seems far away, lost somewhere in the maze of channels.

"No more watching football games all weekend," Jim replies.

"You got a house. You going to get a woman for it one of these days?" Bob asks.

"I don't know. I like things the way I've got them."

"You're too fussy."

"Not like Sammy. He's not fussy. Hey, Sammy, what happened to Boots? She still play her guitar for you?"

"Nah."

"C'mon, you skinny little runt," Bob says, "Give us your life story."

Instead of replying, Sammy coughs spasmodically, then recites, "One times one is one, two times two is two, three times three is nine."

"Two times two isn't two," Jim says.

"You come down here on holidays. Thanksgiving, Christmas, during the summer. Tell us the attraction."

"I can't keep my feet down," Sammy says. "They keep floating."

"Hang onto the tree," Jim says. "It'll keep you steady."

"Mom," Sammy mumbles, but the others don't hear him.

"Sometimes," Jim continues, "I wake up at two in the morning and go around touching things. I say this is mine, and this is mine, and nobody can take it away from me. Never again."

"Mom," Sammy says but his lips don't move. "Are we going to stay here?"

"We're going to get a house in the suburbs and have two kids," Bob says.

"Mom," Sammy says, "I like it here. Do you know they have community dinners in the fall? There's a hockey rink and a dance hall in the park. All the guys go duck hunting in the fall."

Gradually, the cold silences them except for their coughing. The moon, hard and pale, inches its way up the sky. They see lights and boats and people and scenes from their childhood and strange beasts that rise from the depths, so that when finally a light sweeps across the red cap, then returns, and a Mountie says "I've found them," they aren't sure that he is any different from their earlier hallucinations, that the boat pushing up to them is any more substantial than the hundreds they have dreamt.

There are two men riding the water above them. They are part of a search party that has been looking ever since the empty duck boat drifted into a blind. The two men grasp Jim under the arms, drag him onto the gunwale, catch hold of his belt and heave him up. Then one of them jumps into the water, finds footing and helps lift Bob so that his companion can pull him to safety. He turns to Sammy, who does not know they are there. Sammy, who is lost in darkness, Sammy, who thinks he is diving at the Eddyville dock in moonlight, searching the rocky bottom for something he has lost. His head is shaking uncontrollably, and when, at last, they manage to break his hold on the submerged willow and get him into the boat, his whole body begins to jerk, and as the boat turns across the black water toward land, he thrashes about in one last frenzy, then is still. And he's naked, diving from the little dock, down and down through the image of the moon into the darkness, knowing that if he holds his breath just one moment longer, kicks hard one more time, he will find the brilliant stones for which he has been endlessly searching.

Snow

==

Snow had started falling that morning, dropping over everything like a gauze curtain, isolating objects in a white haze. Gradually, the rough, bare patches of cinder and the wiry tufts of grass along the edge of the railway tracks were covered.

"Rabbits?" Cliff queried, opening the door of the railway station to peer across the platform. A crest of poplars less than a hundred yards away was blurred and indistinct.

"In this weather?" Arlene replied. She rubbed the heel of her hand over the window to clear the mist from the glass. On the other side of the tracks, the slab fence with its broken and tilted boards looked like a line of lost cripples struggling blindly through the storm.

"This is the weather for it. No wind. Fresh snow so we can see new tracks."

Arlene hesitated. Just after breakfast, they had fought, not loudly or violently but with a sudden flurry of words as sharp and painful as bits of jagged glass. It had hurt them both and left them wary of attempting to bridge the silence, a silence that the sullen clouds and grey light had reinforced.

For the last two weeks, their days had been filled with indefinable exasperations, making them irritable with each other and quick to take offence at even so slight a thing as a tone of voice. Being alone so much, Arlene was certain, had a lot to do with it, but it was not the only reason. Worry over their too rapidly eroding savings weighed on them both.

When they had been crowded into a small city apartment overflowing with oil painting and pottery equipment, the idea of buying an abandoned railway station in the country had seemed an excellent idea. There would be no end of space: snug living quarters and lots of storage area, but best of all, a large waiting room, which, with its black, pot-bellied stove and windows on three sides, could be turned into a studio large enough for both of them. During the summer, the highway location would allow them a prime display area for their work. Passing motorists, on their way to their summer cottages, would be good prospects. Then there had been the added benefit of being on the edge of a small town. While they would have the necessary privacy for their work, they would be able to walk to the grocery store, the movie house, the skating rink. Expenses would be minimal.

Now, if anything, they had too much privacy. The local farmers never came to town except when driven from their homes by the need to purchase groceries or to have broken equipment repaired. The townspeople were reticent to the point of being rude. Suspicious of anyone who painted pictures instead of working, especially pictures that contained no recognizable objects, they remained aloof.

In the city, Arlene and Cliff had both fought for and cherished every second they had for their work. Now, they brooded through weekends, hoping every car that used their parking lot to turn around in was bringing visitors. What made it even more difficult was the knowledge that their plan to spend a full year as artists was going awry.

She drew her hand away from the window and wiped it on her jeans. Rather than turn around, she studied Cliff's image in the blurred window.

"Okay," she consented, without any softening of her voice that would indicate she wanted to make peace.

They pulled on their parkas and their mukluks. The mukluks, soft, smoky-smelling moosehide boots so flexible and light that they were no heavier than a warm sock, were their only real extravagance since coming to Eddyville. Cliff's mukluks, because they were men's, were lavishly decorated with beads. The leggings were fitted with red and green felt. At the end of the drawstring that held them tightly to the leg were two orange and blue pompoms. Arlene's were plainer, more practical, their leggings undecorated except for a band of arctic hare.

Cliff took their twenty-two calibre rifles down from the rack and spilled a cascade of small bronze shells into her palm. They went outside to stand under the protection of the wide eaves. Snow had come late to Manitoba this year, but it was now falling in earnest. The grove of trees had disappeared and the fence was only a faint image, as though it had been brushed onto white paper with pale grey water. They waited in silence, adjusting to the loneliness of the enclosing snow. For Arlene it was a good feeling, a clean feeling, as though her mind was being swept clear of complexities in preparation for the task before them.

Arlene liked to hunt. That fact had surprised her. She had been born and brought up in the city, only making quick weekend trips to the country for swimming or barbecuing, rituals that could as easily have been performed in the suburbs. When they had first come to Eddyville, she had been nervous about the empty fields and thick groves of trees, but they had inexorably drawn her to them.

At first, she had walked the railway line, secure in the rigidity of the metal rails and heavy crossties. Then, a little at a time, she struck out, exploring the fence lines, surprising herself with a keen sense of direction. She had noticed the crudely lettered sign in the grocery store offering the rifles for sale and had talked Cliff into going to see about them. In the afternoons they had sat on the edge of the platform, shooting tins off the crossbars of the fence. Then, rather than buy dressed rabbits at ninety cents a pound from the lady who brought eggs and, occasionally, scrawny chickens good only for soup, they had begun to hunt.

Cliff took the lead as they started off, following the railway spur that in clear weather branched off in a long graceful curve. It provided an easy path to an old cut in the bush where irregularly spaced brush piles formed low, domed lodges for small animals. Instinctively, she watched for landmarks, but those that did appear were pale and insubstantial, hardly recognizable. The rails were covered over, and Cliff kept to the tracks more by touch than sight.

At the barbed wire fence that marked the end of the railway property, they rested, squatting on their haunches, their rifles across their knees. A slight wind had risen so they sat with their backs to it, facing each other at an angle.

The hood of Cliff's parka shadowed his face, but Arlene could see snowflakes that had gathered along his eyebrows. He was fair, with a child's pink skin and hair so blond that it was nearly white. His cheeks were bright red from the cold and his exertion. He was tall, over six feet, and had the loose build and large hands of a basketball player but none of the grace. Although he was twenty-seven, he still retained traces of adolescent awkwardness. Arlene was dark and slight. When they had first met, Cliff had thought she might be partly Spanish. To keep up the fantasy, he liked her to wear bright skirts and shawls.

"It's good to get out," Cliff ventured. After they quarrelled, he always tried to establish dialogue with indisputable statements. She knew that if she did not reply, he would begin a monologue of truisms.

"We've got to do something about getting jobs," she answered, refusing to make peace until the point was settled. Usually, to her annoyance, he found some way of avoiding painful decisions. For once, she was determined to see something through to the end.

"We've only got a thousand dollars left," she continued, stubbornly clinging to her morning's argument, "and five months to go before the tourists come. Even when they do, we have no guarantee that they will buy anything. We can't survive on two hundred a month. The heat alone comes to fifty." She did not mention that she had quit using the kiln to keep the electricity bill down, but they both knew it.

They had been over it all before, trying to avoid the facts, making up improbable schemes, pinning their hopes on sales that did not come, grants that were turned down. An open house for the local people, with paintings and pots priced at little more than cost, had brought the minister, a sincere middle-aged man who had taken an art course as an undergraduate, and five shy high school girls who giggled at everything. Except for what they drank themselves, the coffee Arlene had prepared went untouched. The minister, not knowing how to escape gracefully, bought a teapot with a rattan handle.

After that, she had made a set of posters offering private lessons. She had tacked them up at the school, the general store and the skating rink. A lady in a blue dress with a flowered hat had stopped by. She had not wanted to use the wheel. She had wanted to decorate greenware.

Cliff sat still, the snow gathering in the crevices of his jacket, his face empty. Arlene felt that if she reached out and pushed him with the tip of her rifle, he would topple rigidly to the ground and lie unmoving as the snow covered him.

"We're going to have to see about teaching school," she said.

At last, it was out. Before this, they had always stopped short of the conclusion, managed somehow to avoid admitting that they would have to be what they had promised themselves they would never become. There was always a need for art teachers. The schools sucked them in, chewed them into cripples and spit them out so fast that the supply was never large enough to meet the demand. One friend of theirs had lasted three months. Another had lasted a week.

During their years in art school, Cliff and Arlene had mocked the Saturday Morning Specials, the public school teachers who had once wanted to be artists. Every Saturday morning they came for studio classes, frighteningly unsure of themselves, as if they were ready at any moment to be rebuked. After working dispiritedly or desperately for four hours, they disappeared again, wrapped in a defeated silence. As Arlene had watched their savings begin to run out, the ghosts of all those ruined ambitions had haunted her.

"Let's hunt rabbits," Cliff said, at last.

He still had not looked at her. She had the feeling, at times, that he resented her, as though he felt that if he were by himself, he would somehow manage, conveniently forgetting that she had contributed more than half the capital for the venture. She did not mention it, for as blunt as she had been about the need for jobs, she did not want to set between them the question of who earned what.

Before them was a brush pile. They circled it, looking for tracks, then Cliff said, "Jump on it," and she heard the sharp, metallic sound of his rifle being cocked.

She tensed, then kicked the brush pile with all her strength. The white dome cracked, then dissolved, revealing a crosshatch of tangled branches. Expecting, at most, one rabbit, Cliff was rendered helpless when two appeared. He paused, unable to decide, then, too late, swung for the one on his right, wasting a bullet on the already invisible figure.

At the next pile, he kicked and Arlene stood ready, but the jackrabbit sprang directly at her. She was so startled that she did not have time to shoot.

As they moved from brush pile to brush pile, they paid no attention to where they were going, not that it mattered, for once having crossed the fence there were no landmarks to guide them. The ground, the sky, were all white. Behind them, their footprints filled in within moments. Arlene paused, suffering a sense of vertigo, wondering if she should not go back to the house. Her mother would have, she thought. Her mother would have stayed in the kitchen washing the dishes, baking cookies, while her father would have gone out there beyond the kitchen window to do whatever it was that men did. Her mother and father had been married for forty years, and that was how it worked.

At the fourth brush pile, Arlene backed away, squatted, holding her rifle loosely with her right hand. The rifle was small, no longer than her arm and so light that she could hold it easily in one hand. When the rabbit bounded to the left, she swung the rifle in a smooth arc, her arm straight, her index finger pointing along the barrel. She fired automatically and the rabbit, hit from so close, was knocked sideways. With a feeling of satisfaction, she picked up the warm body and tied its legs to her belt with a piece of cord.

Annoyed with her success, Cliff said, "Maybe you could see if the local school board would hire an art teacher. There's no use my asking. I don't have as many education courses as you."

Stiffly, she replied, "I had thought we might both work part-time," and started away.

Angrily, she searched for another brush pile. When she found one, she looked behind her for Cliff. With a surge of fear, she realized he had refused to follow her. Her first impulse was to cry out and run back the way she had come, but she caught herself. There was no need for panic, she thought, her lips just forming the words. Although the station and the town were not visible, she knew they were there. In spite of the rising wind, it was not particularly cold and she was warmly dressed. She rested, gaining control of herself, getting used to the idea that she was alone.

She made herself realize that there was not endless, frightening space around her. On either side, even though she could not see them, were straight rows of trees.

She took fifty steps in one direction. Finding nothing, she stopped, turned and started forward at a right angle.

When she had gone thirty steps, the tree line materialized. The panic that had surged inside her subsided. The worst that could happen was that she might go in the wrong direction, but even if she did it was not serious. Going west would bring her to the highway. She would then have to turn around and go back until she reached the fence. What was important was to keep calm, to remain in charge.

She rested again, her back to the wind. Her hand went to the rabbit, feeling its fur under her mitten. Its being there gave her a feeling of confidence.

All at once, she heard Cliff call her name. His voice, muffled by the snow and distorted by the wind, was just barely recognizable, and it was impossible to tell from which direction the sound came.

She went to reply, then did not, settling into herself, preparing for the walk back. Cliff's voice grew louder and louder, then fainter. Once, he came close enough so that in the half-light she was able to make out movement, to discern a dim form robbed of any recognizable identity, but still she said nothing.

Instead, she sat motionless, her head turned sideways inside her parka hood, as he called across a vast and unbridgeable distance.

Circus

We began saving our nickels and dimes the day after the posters went up on the telephone poles. We hunted bottles along the highway's edge until our hair was thick with dust. We stole old car batteries from behind garages and sold them to the itinerant scrap dealer who drove up and down back lanes in his green Ford truck. We peddled George's fish fillets to the campers. One pound of pickerel fillets for fifty cents. Our share was a nickel. We cut grass. When we relaxed at the beach or the park, we had terse, distracted conversations.

"Elephants. There are always elephants."

"And tigers."

And lions. And clowns. And women, although we weren't really sure where women fitted in. We were in grade seven and wouldn't have thought of women except for the poster. On it, there was the picture of a woman on horseback. There'd never been a circus in town before, so we took our knowledge from the Saturday matinees.

"And snakes," Gerald said. Big snakes that wound around women's bodies. We said we didn't believe him, but he was a year older and his father had been in the navy during the war and he knew things the rest of us hadn't even dreamed of. That night I had nightmares about a monstrous snake trying to swallow me, and all the reassurances I'd received from endless Tarzan comics in which he regularly killed anacondas with his hunting knife didn't come to my rescue. High-wire acts, I said. That was the comic books again. Archie went to a circus once, and he and

Veronica and Betty watched acrobats flying through the air with death-defying bravery.

The circus was going to be in the big field directly across from my parents' house. The field was a square block of flat grassy land, where during the long summer evenings we played rugby or baseball.

All over town, in pickle jars or in the bottom of socks, nickels and dimes and quarters were piling up. Every day, without planning it, coming from swimming at the big dock or from fishing for perch, we gathered before the one large, full-colour poster that hung in Bjarnason's store window. Here the lion was caught in mid-leap, the white horse trotted boldly (the girls who infrequently joined us were more interested in the lady bareback rider in a short white dress, with feathers in her hair). I even took to stroking the days off the calendar, drawing an x through each day as if to say thank goodness that is over.

In the evenings, when we'd finished playing baseball or football, a peculiar silence would fall over us, as if, collectively, we were all imagining how the field—which had always been just as it was, flat, covered in grass, edged on three sides with ditches from which the occasional muskrat emerged, marked in one corner with a chicken-wire backstop and our wooden bases—would become transformed. It seemed impossible. There was nothing there now, except us and the swallows chasing mosquitoes—the easy silence as we waited for our mothers to call us in to get ready for bed.

No one knew where it started, but on the day before the circus was to arrive, a rumour ran among us like a grass fire, whipped this way and that, confirmed and denied a hundred times. The circus would hire kids to help them set up the tents. They would pay with tickets to the matinee.

"The freak show," Robert said. "That's what I want to see. They've got two-headed babies and a lizard man and a bearded woman."

The circus vehicles were already parked on the field when I woke up. Just outside my bedroom window there were elephants—well, one elephant—and he was being used to help set up the tents. I couldn't wait for breakfast. I dressed and ran across the field to offer my services. Others were there ahead of me, but I still got a job pulling ropes tight. Three or four of us would heave on the rough hemp while one of the men drove a peg into the ground.

Secretly, we watched for the clowns, the bareback riders, the magicians, the performers, but they were nowhere to be seen. Three horses were tethered to the side of a truck. There were dogs. Three lions in cages. There was a dwarf. I stared at him so hard I walked into a large crate. We weren't much help but we were given yellow tickets anyway. By noon, five tents had been set up and all the feverish activity stopped. The circus people vanished into their trailers.

The matinee was wonderful. The tent put-er-uppers were hardly recognizable in their costumes and their makeup. They glittered with sequins as they rode and strode about the ring. The acrobats flew back and forth as recklessly as anyone could ever have hoped. Before the end of the afternoon performance, I would have sacrificed parents, house, baseball games, everything, to run away with the circus. When I stumbled home, it was not so much individual scenes that filled my head but a whirling, ever-changing pattern of colours. It was like trying to remember having looked into a kaleidoscope and not being able to recall individual patterns but intense, confusing colour. At supper time, I was frantic with the fear that my father would be late from work and that we would miss the evening performance.

By the time we got to the circus, the crowd was bigger than any I'd ever seen before. You could tell the farmers in from the country with their families. The men were burned brown with a band of white skin where their hair had been cut. The boys wore freshly pressed checked shirts. The women wore dresses and the girls wore blouses and skirts with crinolines. Even the fishermen had squeezed into suits in which all the fold marks could be seen.

After the show, my parents wandered away to visit the rest of the circus, to talk with everyone they knew.

Just inside one tent a table had materialized, and on it, a man with a checkered vest was manipulating three walnut shells. He kept revealing and hiding a pea and challenging anyone to find it. The men were standing, suspicious, in a semicircle, and behind them there was a semicircle of their wives. No one came forward until one of the boys who worked at the fish shed put down ten dollars. There was a stir. Wages were a dollar an hour, and most people who worked for themselves didn't make that. Ten dollars would buy a week's groceries. The man behind the table moved his hands back and forth, switching the shells, revealing the pea then hiding it, but never so fast that I could not see where it was. Finally he stopped, and the boy pointed to the middle shell. The man turned over the shell, and there was the pea. He passed over ten dollars. With that, one of the farmers stepped forward, and he won a dollar. Another won two dollars. The farmers pulled worn bills from their pockets, bills they had been hoarding all winter for seeds and tools, and their eyes never left the shells. I was going to put down my five dollars when my grandfather caught my hand and shook his head. It's there, Bill, I said. I saw it. When the shell was turned over it wasn't there, and my grandfather dragged me out of the tent.

I saw it, I said. It wasn't there, Bill said, it was between his fingers. The Mounties should put a stop to it.

The Mounties, I realized, were standing at the back of the crowd, watching. We watched them watch the game until they turned around and walked away.

I had seen everything there was to see in the tents and, out of curiosity, threaded my way among the trailers, being rewarded by a glimpse of a clown taking off his makeup, of a trainer prodding the lions into separate cages. At the back of the farthest tent, I discovered a narrow stage. Beneath a single light that hung from a pole, a woman dressed in a red costume covered with sequins and feathers was pacing back and forth. A barker, a short fat man wearing a checked jacket and white pants, was calling her the hootchie-kootchie queen, and every time he said it, a narrow man who needed a shave would bang on a drum and the woman would wiggle and shake and slide one shoulder out of her top or lift up her dress. Miss Veronica, the barker said, had acted on the London stage, had been at the Old Vic, had played Ophelia, Desdemona, and now had consented to come all the way to Canada to share her many talents. She was, I thought, glamorous. She had high-heeled red shoes, a dress that shimmered like jewels, dark hair piled high with feathers, rings on every finger. A dollar to see the dance of the seven veils, the dance that drove King Herod mad, an opportunity to understand temptation, just in here, the barker called. After all the men had gone in, I offered the drummer a dollar. He was also the ticket taker.

He started to wave me away, but the barker said, let him in, he might learn something. The space was small and crowded and smelled of sweat and anticipation and there was a raised stage so Miss Veronica's feet were at the level of the spectators' waists. The barker played a guitar and the ticket seller was transformed again to a drummer. Miss Veronica began to dance, undoing buttons and wiggling suggestively. In a couple of minutes she was down to what today would be considered a modest two-piece bathing suit. That's the hootchie-kootchie, the barker said, but those of you who want to know the secret of the seven veils will pay three dollars more. All will be revealed. A number of men groaned and complained loudly but no one left. The drummer took their money; he gave me his thumb for the doorway.

Outside, I skirted the tent until I found a small rip. By standing on tiptoe I could see Miss Veronica. As the music started again she began to twist and turn, and one coloured veil after another floated through the air. After a time she took off her top and held it up to a round of applause. As the men shifted about, I saw her breasts, the first I remembered seeing except for women nursing babies in our kitchen, and then there was a silence from the men and she held up the bottom of the suit. I couldn't see anything more because of all the men in the way, but the music became faster and louder and Miss Veronica appeared and disappeared from my view and then the guitar player threw something to her. Now, Miss Veronica will demonstrate her own special talent for you, he shouted, then went back to playing, and she did something that made all the men laugh but I couldn't see what it was, then one of the men yelled, I'll give you twenty bucks to teach my old lady that trick, and she grabbed his hat and threw it back to him, then the music stopped and the drummer pulled a curtain in front of her. Some of the men groaned, but the barker said, there'll be another show in one hour.

I'd read about Salome and the seven veils at Sunday school, but I'd never thought of it before as being done by a real person, and I felt a sudden sense of shock and wondered if it had been like this, crowded with men, noisy and hot. That night I dreamt of Salome, though in my dream she was not the silent, decorous young woman illustrated in my Bible storybook, but Miss Veronica, and while she danced, a tray was brought in. When it was turned toward me, it was not the head of John the Baptist but mine, and I jerked from sleep, crying.

In the morning, the circus was gone. They had vanished as secretly as they had come. My mother and father were already up, and I heard my mother comment on how the circus had disappeared, leaving no trace, and my father said, yes, they knew how to make a quick exit. I slipped outside looking for souvenirs. but there weren't any, only deep ruts gouged into our baseball diamond and, where the animals had been chained, piles of shit already covered with flies.

The Couch

Cramped between her husband and her father-in-law, Ruby set her jaw and stared fiercely toward town.

"The old couch is good enough," Ansford said. "It's just for sitting."

"It's got the spring through," she replied to her husband before she could stop herself. She had resolved to argue no more. They had argued since Christmas. Arguing was delaying and she was through delaying. Her mind was made up.

"You can sit to one side," Jacob countered. "You don't got to sit on the spring."

On either side, trees rose toward them in a black line, then rushed past with a jerk as though they had been attached to a string that somebody had pulled. Ruby had not been to town for twelve months and the sameness of the road depressed her. She had remembered the countryside as having more variety.

There was no traffic. They had not seen a car since they had left the island. Nor were there any houses or farms. Occasionally, a slash in the thick bush would mark the way to one of the temporary lumber camps that dotted the area. Now that the ground had thawed, most of the camps were abandoned. A few had caretakers, men who had become so bushed they could not bear going to town. When she had first been married to Ansford, Ruby had gone with him to deliver potatoes and fish to a camp. It had been a poor kind of place—a rough clearing dotted with stumps. There had been two bunkhouses on skids, piles of sawdust. There had been a caretaker, a little man with a wooden leg he had carved himself. He wore his pant leg folded back at the knee, and he had painted a blue pant leg with a wide cuff, a red sock and a black shoe on the wooden stump. When they had come, he had hidden behind a sawdust pile for five minutes, coming out only when Ansford held up a mickey of whiskey. After three or four drinks, he had invited them into his caboose. Standing along one wall were half a dozen legs, some with green pants, some with gray, some with galoshes, others with rubber boots. The sight had given her quite a turn. She was not, Ruby had told herself then, going to become like that.

"Aren't you going awfully fast?" she asked, as Ansford pulled the truck out of a skid that nearly put them into the ditch. The tie rods were worn and the truck, at the slightest excuse, was inclined to wander.

The roads were barely wide enough for two cars to pass. The edges rose toward the centre to form a convex surface. No matter how much gravel was dumped during the winter, the moment the spring thaw began, the piles of stone sank from sight.

Ansford was too busy wrestling the wheel to reply. Jacob jerked his thumb at the ceiling.

"Going to rain," he said, as though she could not see for herself. Clouds lay in overlapping bands like windrows of grey stone. "We should go home." Raising his voice to be heard over the gravel drumming like hail on the underside of the truck, he repeated, "Going to rain. Better go home."

Ruby leaned forward, her face composed. She pretended she did not hear him. Ansford glanced at his father, but the truck immediately swerved toward the left and he had to haul on the wheel. Although they were not long on the road, his eyes had taken on a wild look and his dark hair stuck out in spikes.

"Go back," her father-in-law intoned. Ruby sniffed. She refused to have anything to do with him unless he had his teeth in. He had a long, lean face that was the duplicate of his son's except that it ended in a collapsed mouth that looked like a shell crater. His false teeth bulged in his shirt pocket. Despite her efforts to get him to wear them regularly, he stubbornly kept them in a sandwich bag and refused to wear them except for special occasions.

Ruby secretly studied Ansford's face. Ever since she had first met her father-in-law, she had watched her husband's teeth surreptitiously, finding excuses to look in his mouth. He had already lost two teeth and that worried her. One had become infected for no reason. The other had broken while he was cracking hazelnuts. Certain that this was the beginning of a dental disaster, at night when Ansford was asleep, she sometimes rolled back his lip and inspected his teeth as carefully as those of a prize horse.

The three of them had started their trip at five o'clock that morning. She had been so determined to get an early start that she had gone downstairs at four to sit beside the door, her suitcase at her knee. For the trip, she wore rubber boots, slacks, two sweaters and a parka. In her suitcase she had a dress, a hat with two blue plastic daisies, black shoes and a cloth coat. She also had clothes for Ansford and Jacob.

Her husband and father-in-law had come downstairs reluctantly. Ansford had come first, Jacob muttering behind him. Normally, both of them sat at the kitchen table, but for the last week, as her determination to buy a new couch had become apparent, they had taken to sitting on the old couch to show her how much wear was still in it. She had not given them an opportunity to delay her but had, on the stroke of five, the agreed-upon time, picked up her suitcase and started for the dock. Ansford and Jacob had trailed a couple of yards in her wake.

Neither of them was much good at hurrying at the best of times, but they had hung back like two stone anchors that she had to drag forward with every step. There were no lights in the five houses they passed. She could hear her own breathing and the swish of her boots on the grass. The lake, in this hour before dawn, was flat and dark as asphalt. She climbed down to the skiff, took her place on the middle seat and sat stiffly, waiting, like a queen about to be transported to another country.

The wind they made as they crossed the half-mile to the mainland was bitter. The ice had broken up only the week before, and rafted ice still stood in piles along the shore like a line of hunchbacked dwarves. As the island faded, the mainland appeared, a solider darkness against the purple sky. Their truck was parked among a dozen vehicles owned by the people who lived on the island. There was no ferry service. Anyone who did not have a boat had to sit and flash his car lights until he was noticed. Then someone came to pick him up.

"We're going on a fool's errand," her father-in-law had said as he climbed into the truck.

When the time came, she thought, burying him would be a chore. While they were carrying the casket to the graveyard, he would still manage to mutter complaints about the inconvenience.

Dawn had been a thin red line enameled to the tops of the trees on the far shore. The line of colour between the sombre darkness of sky, land and water lasted only a few minutes; then thick, solid-looking clouds had filled the gap. In the gloom, lined with forest on both sides, covered over with low clouds so heavy they seemed about to fall, the road might have been the bottom of a trench.

Ruby looked up as a flurry of rain scattered over the windshield. There was a pause that was just long enough to give them hope the rain would hold off for another hour. Thunder shook the side windows of the truck. Before the noise had faded, rain poured down. Ahead, the road darkened. Ansford flicked on the windshield wipers. He jerked his foot off the gas pedal and let the truck glide in neutral until they had slowed to twenty.

Neither of them, she thought with a small flush of resentment as she looked at the mud, ever remembered to take off his shoes at the door. It was a constant source of aggravation. No matter how often she washed the floors, they were never clean. Both men left trails of mud wherever they went. She had tried putting a mat outside the door. When that had not worked, she had added a sign saying "Boots here." She had spread newspaper inside the door. Finally, when it rained, she had taken to making a path of newspaper from the back door to every room in the house. The first time she had done it, they had carefully sidestepped the paper, certain it was for something special.

Ansford and she had met at an upgrading class in Winnipeg. The government was paying them both to attend so that they would not be counted as unemployed. For Ansford, squeezed between a bad fishing season and the need for new nets, it was a chance to get cash money. For Ruby, it was a chance to get off her feet. She had been a cashier at Safeway for five years. Nine months of the year, a cold wind blew across the floor every time a customer came in or went out. The manager, thinking it would keep the customers' minds off rising grocery prices, insisted that the girls wear short skirts and shoes instead of boots. The constant standing on concrete had covered her calves with a fine mesh of red veins.

Ansford had brought her to the island late one night. Douglas McBrie had taken them across. He had said nothing to either of them, but as she was climbing out of the boat Ruby heard Ansford say, "I got her and a new outboard while I was in the city."

Ansford had told her he had a house and furniture. Her father-in-law came as a surprise. When they arrived, the house was dark and silent. She and Ansford, exhausted from a long day on the road, had gone straight to bed. He had fallen asleep but she, overtired and excited by the unfamiliarity of the house that was to be her home, had been unable to sleep. Restless and not wanting to wake Ansford, she had started to go downstairs. Jacob had been standing in his nightshirt in the hallway, a tall, thin ghost with knock knees. She had been wearing a blue flannel nightgown and had her hair set with pink plastic curlers. Jacob and she had stood rooted in place. The look that crept onto his face as the shock passed made her feel like the whore of Babylon. Wordlessly, she had fled, shutting the door behind her and dragging a chest of drawers against it.

The next morning, Ansford explained to Jacob that he had married. Jacob had nodded, but his eyes and the pensive set of his mouth revealed that he did not really believe it. Even the marriage certificate did not erase his lingering doubt. She and Ansford had been married twelve years, but Ruby was sure that Jacob, somewhere deep behind his eyes, believed they were living in sin.

The truck began to jerk. Ruby looked up. "What's the matter?" she asked sharply.

"Mud," Jacob yelled. His hearing was not good. To hear his own voice, he had to shout.

Ansford was pressed so close to the steering wheel that he seemed to be impaled upon it.

Ruby braced her feet on the floor and raised herself from the seat so that she could see herself in the mirror. She had carefully set her hair the night before, but already the violent motion of the truck was making it untidy. Swaying with the truck, she used her fingers to comb her hair into place. She prided herself on not letting her standards go. Many of the women did. They looked fine, but the moment they got married it was as though some tightly twisted rubber band inside them was snipped and they began to fall apart. Every Friday, she religiously set her hair and changed the bed sheets. Some women she knew never combed their hair, never mind set it, and changed the linens every spring. She had told Ansford right after they married that she could not live like that.

Jacob guarded his sheets as if they were jewels. At first she had fought with him, but gradually, she had learned to have her way without conflict. She simply waited until he left the house, and since none of the doors, including the outer ones, had locks, she went into his room and remade his bed. Occasionally, if his liver was bothering him, he still berated her, beating his fist on the table, shouting, "You leave my sheets alone, you hear! They're fine. You'll just wear them out." Of late, she had noticed that his voice was no longer sharpened by conviction.

Instructed by the country memories of parents who had moved to the city when she was only two, she had come prepared for the wrong battle. Life on the island was not endless visiting in other people's kitchens. Work seldom ceased. Leisure was idleness forced upon people by blizzards. The men cut, repaired, dug, ploughed and fished endlessly. Their wives, inundated with children, never gave over cooking, washing and mending.

Ansford geared down to second. The truck, like a cow that has tried to dodge one way, then another, and failed to escape the drover's switch, settled into a steady run. Ruby opened her purse. It was the shape and size of a shopping bag and made of purple plastic. She took out a round mirror so she could check her makeup. Her face was broad as a pumpkin. Although she constantly dieted, she was still heavy. Hard work had settled her flesh downward like buckshot in a cloth bag.

Jacob's left arm was flung along the back of the seat. He gripped the metal rail fiercely. His long legs were stretched out, and his right foot jerked up and down every time the truck began to skid. His face was strained.

Ruby leaned toward him and held the mirror in front of his face. "Put in your teeth," she yelled in his ear. "You don't want to get killed looking like that."

He jerked his head around like a hawk and tried to stare down his nose at her, but he could not keep his eyes off the road. He could stand in an open boat five miles from land with waves twenty feet tall flinging him about like a cork while he picked fish out of his nets, but he left the island so seldom that each journey took all his courage. Having to ride over bad roads made it worse.

"We got to go back," he shouted. "It ain't worth it to have a new couch."

Out of the corner of her eye, Ruby saw Ansford sneak a glance at her. She knew that if she showed even a moment's weakness, he would turn around and race back home.

"Keep going," she ordered. She was glad she was two years older than he. If she had not been, she would not have had the sense to know that he needed to be told what to do.

"I can't take much more of this," Ansford said. He was holding the wheel so hard that he looked as if he were going to pull it loose. He did not drive much, and when he did, he preferred to travel in the centre of the road at thirty miles an hour. At such times, he sat as far back on the seat as he could, his chest thrown out and his head tipped up so that he was just seeing under the sun visor.

"I got to stop," he said, his voice a defeated whine. Ahead, a driveway made a shallow loop nearly parallel with the road. A tall gas pump with a round glass top like a fish bowl sat in the centre of the driveway. On the edge of the bush, a low green building squatted close to the ground. Ansford parked beside a black Chevrolet with orange ball fringe on all the windows.

They stopped at the door and, leaning in, their heads pressed together like balls, studied the interior. A naked light bulb burned over a single pool table. A group of eight Indians were frozen into position around the green felt, their eyes not looking anywhere, their ears listening to every sound. Ansford led the way to a counter with four stools.

"Bad day to be out," a fat man in tweed pants and a white shirt said. On the pocket someone had embroidered *Jimmy*. The left corner of his mouth and his left eyelid drooped. The last part of each word he said was slurred.

"Whad he say?" Jacob demanded, rifling his pockets for change.

"He said it was a bad day out," Ansford said. Ruby was sitting between them so Ansford had to lean steeply to one side to get his mouth close to his father's ear.

The Indians had started to play pool again, but when Ansford shouted, they froze into place, shining under the light like pieces of old walnut furniture.

"A bad day," Jacob repeated, nodding to himself, his eyes reflective. He turned to Ruby, thrust his face close to hers and bellowed, "It's a bad day for being out. We should turn around and go home."

"Coffee," Ruby said. "Black."

"Whad she say?" Jacob asked Ansford.

The Indians still had not moved.

"Coffee," Ansford replied at the top of his voice.

Jacob nodded vigorously. "Me, too."

Jimmy brought their order for them, dropping the heavy white crockery with a clatter.

"You must be Jimmy," Ruby said.

The fat man shook his head. "I'm Bill."

"Whad he say?" Jacob asked.

"My name's Bill," the fat man shouted.

They all studied his pocket. He looked down.

"Got these at an auction," he explained, raising his voice as if he were talking to a multitude. "They all got different names on them."

"It says Jimmy," Jacob insisted.

Before Bill could explain again, Ruby said, "I don't remember you from last year."

"Christmas," he replied. "Under new ownership. Had a sign. Wind blew it down." He shouted each phrase so that Jacob could hear.

"You from the city?" Ruby asked. He nodded. "I seen your white shirt and I knew." She shot a glance full of reproval at Ansford. "My husband's got a white shirt. He won't wear it but once a year."

Ansford leaned closer to his coffee. He had spread his elbows on the counter and was counting the different kinds of candy bars. There were five kinds he had not eaten.

"I'd give a dollar to go back home right now," Jacob declared.

"You'd think we made him come." Ruby pressed her lips together in mild indignation the way she might with a child. "He
complains all the time, but if we leave him alone for half an hour,
he comes looking for us."

"The road's bad farther on," Bill said.

"You seen these?" Jacob asked. He dug into his jacket pocket
and held out a rooster carved from a forked stick. "I sold lots of
these. Dollar apiece."

Bill saw Ruby looking at the name on his pocket. "Tomorrow,
I'll be Norman. The day after that, Robert."

"If you bought five for a dollar each," Jacob said, peering at
Bill's face, trying to see if there was a flicker of interest, "you
could sell them for a dollar seventy-five."

"How do you know who you are?" Ansford burst out. "Every
day you've got a different name."

Jacob was holding the rooster between his thumb and forefinger, twirling it around so that all its good points would be
revealed. Bill turned back and nearly got the rooster in the eye.

"He likes to whittle," Ruby said. "Finish up," she said to Ansford. Ansford was trying to make his coffee last as long as possible.

Bill reached a large hand under the counter and drew out a
brown envelope. "Would you deliver this to the garage? It's a
cheque for some car parts. They won't send any more until they
get paid."

Ruby slid off the stool. "Not much business here." She took
the envelope and squashed it into her jacket pocket.

"Suits me." He folded his hands over this stomach. "Had a
stroke. Can't do more than a little."

"I wish you luck." She said it with solemnity, the way she
might to someone who had declared he was going to jump off a
cliff and try to fly.

"I got a pension."

Ruby adjusted her head scarf and started for the door. Behind
her, Bill called, "It ain't much but everybody's got to have something to keep him going."

They hurried through the rain that cut across the sky. The
drops fell with such force that the water might have collected

around a centre of lead. Inside the cab, Jacob said petulantly, "If you'd a just waited, I'd a sold him some carving." When he felt unjustly treated, he had a way of drawing his eyebrows together until they nearly touched.

The road was as slick as if it had been greased. Rain fell steadily. The ditches were full. Ruts had become long bands of nearly black water.

Jacob sat deep in thought for the first mile and she thought he was sulking, but all at once he straightened up, looked at them both and said, "He must be hard of hearing. He certainly shouts a lot."

They travelled the next thirty miles in silence. Because of the rain there was nothing to see, and Ruby and Jacob fell into a light doze until Ansford startled them by sharply calling out a warning.

They were approaching a bog. The land on either side of the road was a sea of moss. Full-grown trees were not more than three feet high. When they crossed the edge of the bog, it was as if the truck had been grabbed from behind. Their bodies were flung forward. Ansford gunned the motor. The truck jerked so violently that it felt as if the transmission had been ripped out. Ansford slammed the truck into second, then first. It was no use. The truck slowed; the motor coughed and died. Ruby could feel the wheels sinking.

They sat, staring into the rain. There was nothing before them except empty road and endless forest. On either side of them, there was forest. Behind them, blurred by rain, the trees went on until the road disappeared and the two dark lines converged.

"We can't stay here," she said.

"We're twenty miles from town," Ansford protested.

"We can't go back. We've come too far."

Ansford looked out the rear window. When he turned back, the skin on his face was tight with worry.

"We should of stayed home," Jacob wailed. "I told you. Every year it's the same. The ice goes off the lake and she's got to go town for something."

"Let's go," she said, her voice determined. "Sitting here talking isn't going to get us anywhere."

She gave Ansford a shove with her hip.

"I'm not going," Jacob screamed. "I'm an old man. My legs won't take it."

Ruby gave Ansford another shove. He opened his door and got out. He lifted Ruby's suitcase out of the wooden box on the back of the truck. As they started away, Jacob yelled, once more, "I'm not going. I don't have to go just because you say so."

The rain beat on them as they ploughed through the mud. Mud clung to their boots like paste. Mud splashed up their legs. With every step, Ruby had to pull her foot loose. The ground was a quagmire. Each time she lifted her feet, more mud clung to them. After fifteen minutes her feet were so grotesquely large that she had to stop. Behind her, she heard water splash.

She turned around. Jacob was standing nearly on her heels. His shoulders were hunched together. Water streamed through his thin hair and poured in a steady stream from his nose. Bending over to protect it from the rain, she reached into her purse and took out a second rain cap of clear plastic. She pulled the cap over Jacob's head and tied the bow beneath his chin.

Seeing his dismay, she shouted, "Nobody's going to see you."

Ansford came up to them with sticks of willow that he had cut. He had flattened one end. With these, they pried the mud from their boots.

The rain swept down, engulfing them, breaking over their heads and shoulders like surf.

Ruby tried various strategies. She tried to pick her way carefully, placing her feet where the gravel was thickest. All that happened was that both mud and gravel came up together. She tried walking on the high spots on the theory that the ground would not be so wet. Then, in the hope that the water would wash her boots clean, she walked in the ruts. Nothing worked. After a while, the weight of the mud on each foot was so great that she had to swing her legs stiffly from the hips.

When they reached what she estimated was the second mile, she checked her watch. It was fifteen after twelve and they had eighteen miles to go. She looked back. The truck had disappeared behind a curtain of rain. In front of them was an endless stretch of mud and sodden trees. All she wanted was to reach the town. The thought that they still had eighteen miles to go made her waver. At the moment, if she could have, she might have agreed to return home. Since that was impossible, she forced herself ahead by thinking about lying in bed at the hotel and watching TV.

At one-thirty they had to stop to rest. They had walked the last half-mile on rising ground, and the going had been easier. Now, the ground sloped down again. As she stood looking along the road, Ruby's thigh muscles felt as if they had been pulled loose. Water was seeping through the seams of her jacket.

"We've got to keep going," Ansford said. Shorter and broader than his father, he still looked lean and hard. He was slightly bandy-legged, and his wet trousers clinging to him emphasized the two outward curves. Water dripped from his plaid cap. He took it off and wrung it out.

He was slow to make up his mind, but once he had, there was no stopping him.

They started off again. Lifting her feet hurt so much that Ruby thought of taking off her boots and socks. Less mud, she was sure, would cling to her skin. She rejected the idea because the mud, only recently thawed, was still cold. Her breathing was beginning to be laboured, her breath whistling in her head. She shivered and wished that she had something hot to drink.

Darkness settled over them so gradually that she was not aware of the fading light until she began to find it difficult to see Ansford. Earlier, she had been worried about being caught on the road in the dark. Now, she was too tired to care.

The rain still fell, no longer in torrents, but in a steady, chilling drizzle. Her legs were soaked. Her face was numb.

The walking had turned to stumbling. There were pauses between steps. At last, they stopped and huddled together.

"How far do you think it is?" she asked.

"Ten miles," Ansford replied, "maybe eleven."

"We've walked all day," Jacob cried, his voice thin as a spider web.

They staggered forward for another hour. Ruby's feet, heavy as cast iron, dragged through the mud. When she realized that Jacob no longer was behind her, she called Ansford. They started back. They found Jacob sitting in a rut. Ansford took one arm, Ruby took the other. Between them, they heaved him to his feet. Since he could go no farther, they led him to the edge of the forest. Even here, under a canopy of branches, rain sifted down upon them. They stood dumbly, unable to see, too tired to want to do anything except lie down and rest.

They turned Jacob in a half-circle, positioned him between two saplings rising from a single root. They pushed him down, cramming him between two trunks so that he was firmly held in place. Ruby sat on the left, Ansford on the right. Oblivious to the rain and their aching bodies, they fell asleep.

Ruby woke up cold. She could not feel anything from the waist down, and at first, she was not sure where she was. Her legs were stretched out before her like two dead weights pinning her to the sodden ground. She lifted her left arm to pluck at her parka and tried to pull it more tightly about her. She was, she realized, still leaning against Jacob. His chin rested on his chest. She knew he was still alive because she could see his nose dilate with each breath. Ansford had fallen over and lay on his back, his mouth open. She wondered, her thoughts distant, detached, how it was that he had not drowned. Mercifully, the rain was only a fine mist.

Grasping the tree with one hand, she pulled herself to her knees. Gradually, as she kneaded her legs, the blood came back into them. She dragged herself to her feet. She did not dare let go of the tree. Her suitcase, she noticed, lay beside Ansford's hand. She was glad that she had wrapped all their belongings in plastic.

She reached out with her toe and jabbed Ansford. He did not move. She kicked harder, digging her toe into his ribs. He opened his eyes, lay staring at the clouds, then closed his eyes again. She kicked him hard enough to hurt her big toe.

"Get up," she said. Her throat was so cold that the words were a croak. "You've got to get up." She had never quit shivering and every time she shut her eyes she had the sensation of falling. She knew that she could do nothing without him.

He opened his eyes, coughed twice, rolled over and pushed himself up. He looked as if he had been dug out of a grave. He was covered from head to foot in mud. Pressed into the mud were twigs, leaves, grass, pine needles, even a couple of feathers. His hair was matted, his eyes sunken.

"Jacob," Ruby said. She slapped him on the back. He groaned. She hit him twice more. He stared dumbly, his eyes unfocussed.

They each took an arm, and because they were weak with hunger and cold, they had to strain to pull him free. At first, he was a dead weight. They walked him in a tight circle, around and around in the wet grass. His legs kept collapsing. One moment his legs held him, then they gave out and he dropped to his knees. Each time, grunting, one hand under each armpit, the other braced just above his elbow, they levered him up. It was like walking a horse with severe colic.

"We'd better get going," Ansford said. He picked up the suitcase.

The day before, mud had clung to their boots. Now, the mud was the consistency of tomato soup. With each step, Ruby sank past her ankles. She could think of nothing except being dry and warm and eating platters of food. Gradually, walking warmed her, but her hunger grew into a savage pain. Even that, however, passed into a dull ache. She felt as though she had swallowed a large, smooth stone.

It was noon when they heard a noise like distant thunder. At first, they ignored it. They staggered forward, their bodies lurching from side to side.

Lifting her eyes from the mud, Ruby looked past the rounded hump of Ansford's back. Moving slowly toward them was a tractor. Ansford looked up and stopped. She saw his shoulders settle as though air had been holding them up and had suddenly been released. She thought he might fall down, but instead, he stood wedged in the mud like a fence post. Ruby stopped, grateful not to have to lift her feet again. She could hear Jacob splashing behind her. When he came abreast, she caught his arm sharply.

He had been walking automatically, his body moving independently of any thought. Her fingers on his jacket sleeve stopped him as completely as if someone had turned off a switch. He stood and stumbled, docile as a tamed animal. The tractor churned toward them.

The tractor driver's back was covered in mud kicked up by the chains. He grinned at them, then got down and gave each of them a hand up.

"Bill at Halfway House phoned to say you were bringing some money he owed me. When you didn't arrive, I figured I'd better come looking for you."

"Spent the night in the bush," Ansford replied.

"Looks like it," the driver said and turned the tractor around.

There was no place to sit, so they rode standing, Ruby and Jacob on either side of the driver, Ansford on the hitch. They climbed down in the middle of Main Street. The rain had melted the mud just enough to spread it evenly over them. Jacob still had on Ruby's head cover.

The tractor driver promised to bring in the truck; then Ruby led the way to the hotel. They rented a room with a double bed and had a cot put in for Jacob.

Ruby had a hot shower with her clothes on. When the water running along the bottom of the tub was no longer grey, she peeled off her parka, waited for the water to clear again, then undressed completely. She washed, changed into the clothes she had brought, then helped Jacob into the bathroom. He moved stiffly. He tried to undo his jacket and could not, so she stood him in the tub and turned on the shower. She undid his parka. The warm water started to revive him. She helped him off with his sweater, undid his shirt and pulled it off. She threw everything into the tub to be washed later. He let her pull off his socks, but when she started to undo his pants, he protested. She told him to be quiet or she'd call Ansford to come and hold him still.

When he stood in nothing but his long underwear, she gave him the soap and left.

Ansford lay curled before the door on a wad of old newspapers, which the desk clerk had given them. All the time he waited, he shivered and jerked. Except for his eyes, he was completely caked in mud, and as it dried, it stiffened so that he looked like an unfinished statue.

Ruby laid out their clothes. She did not have much room in the suitcase, but she had managed to bring a change of clothes for each of them, including white shirts for both men.

While Ansford was washing, she took their dirty clothes to the basement of the hotel and washed and dried them. When she went back upstairs, Ansford and Jacob looked scrubbed and brushed. The three of them went to the dining room and ate two platters of ham and eggs each and drank twelve cups of coffee between them. By the time they were finished, they all had a satisfied, glazed look.

Ruby led them down the sidewalk to the Red and White Hardware and Furniture store. A salesman in a brown suit scurried out from behind a small forest of pole lamps. Ruby scanned the room. The salesman, his eyes full of anticipation, his hands washing themselves in little circular motions, darted this way and that.

"I heard you've got a blue couch for sale," Ruby said. "We need a new one."

The salesman lifted himself up on his toes as though he were a ballet dancer and, wobbling, looked across the array of couches. "I've got a nice red one," he said.

"You've got a blue one," Ruby insisted. "With pansies. I heard at Christmas you had it."

"I sold that months ago," he said.

"I wanted blue," Ruby insisted.

The salesman asked her to wait, hurried away and came back in a minute with a catalogue. He pointed out a picture of a blue chesterfield and offered to order it.

"It's not the way I imagined it." Ruby pursed her lips in disapproval.

"I got others," the salesman said.

"No," Ruby answered. "It isn't what I thought." Her decision made, she turned around and herded the two men before her.

"I told you," Jacob whispered indignantly to Ansford. He moved his teeth about with his tongue. "I told you she wouldn't buy it. Every year it's the same." His voice carried all the way to the other side of the street.

Ruby ignored her father-in-law and stood, her hands on her hips, looking with satisfaction up and down Centre Street. It was only a block long, but the stores were deep and contained a host of objects. There were women in town whom she knew well enough to visit, and on Sunday there was a service at the church.

The rain had stopped. The clouds were breaking up to reveal a clear, bright sky. The street, covered with a thin layer of water, looked as if it had been plated with silver. The store signs, swept clean by rain, were bright and shiny.

"All that," Jacob complained, "for nothing." But there was no force in his voice, for he was squinting, trying to read a sign on the movie house. In any case, Ansford was paying him no attention. He had turned halfway around to try to identify the half-dozen men who were sitting in the window of the garage.

"What can't be helped shouldn't be mourned," Ruby said, seeing her reflection in a puddle as shiny as a newly minted silver dollar. She tilted her hat so that the flowers showed to more advantage. "We can't," she added, "go anywhere until the road dries. There's today and tomorrow. We'll just have to make the best of it."

Hans

I

You come to Gamla Stan to pick up a visiting writer and take him on a journey. When you both reach your Volvo, he says, "This is a dream car." You have difficulty getting started because other cars are in the way. As you back up, you have to turn against the flow of traffic. Nothing is easy any more. Repair work is being done on the highway and traffic is stalled. "This will take some time," you say, and put on jazz based on folk music. "Music like this goes back to the roots of things." The writer answers that the countryside is familiar. He recognizes all the roadside plants and points out the common valerian that was used at one time for nervous disorders.

At Sigtuna you are surprised at there being no restriction on parking. "You may stay as long as you need," a villager tells you. The curator, having been informed of the importance of the visiting writer, has kept open the museum. Here are gathered relics from the past. A woman's comb, a piece of jewelry, a bone needle, cloth woven with great care but now tattered. The writer wants you to examine the remnants of domestic life, but you hurry past to descend into the basement where, you say, there is a display from Linnaeus, he who organized the plant kingdom and created both understanding and order. To your surprise, there is a display of bicycles.

When you ask the old man and the young woman who guard these treasures, they deny any knowledge of Linnaeus. The young girl leads you to the door and informs you that the uncle of Olaf Palme excavated here and that the gravel walk is the outline of an early church. It was built at a time of great faith when people turned away from paganism. Everywhere about the yard, although they cannot be seen, are graves.

You lead the writer past the ruins, which are the reason for coming, and are confused by an old wall. He points back to the crumbling structure of a church. Passing a gravestone, you exclaim, "Only twenty-one when she died." The ruins are so dangerous that the doors are barred. This, though you don't know it, is the climax of the trip. You and the writer both seek a way inside, but every entrance is closed with iron rods. When you turn away in despair, the writer draws your attention to a small tree growing high in the crumbling stone. He says, "There is life even in death." A woman who has been watering flowers gets on her bicycle and rides away. You lead the writer to a new church, buy two candles for yourself, one for him.

After coffee and pastry at Aunt Brown's Restaurant, you complain of a headache. You know, from past times, the location of an apothecary. Here, you buy the strongest analgesic possible and swallow it without water. The writer suggests you return to your apartment, but you reply that the journey is not yet complete. At the car, the writer takes your photograph. Behind you is the lake and, just over your right shoulder, a single sailboat with a broken mast.

On the road to the castle at Drottingham, which is a copy of Versailles but much smaller, the trip grows increasingly difficult. The roads are congested. At Drottingham the garden is closed. When you were there with your first wife, whom you loved, you strolled together among the carefully organized hedges. You walk around the outside of the Court Theatre and see, for the first time, actors in the windows putting on makeup, getting ready for their public performance. When you see this, you turn away abruptly, as if it were a tragedy.

II
))) *THE WRITER* (((

I'm a writer staying at the Lord Nelson in Gamla Stan, the old town where Stockholm began. Here, every building is weighted down with history. Because I'm exhausted from studying cathedrals filled with the dead, I sit slumped on a couch. I am waiting for an editor who has promised he will show me everything I need to know. As I wait for the editor to arrive, I think of Lund and the gates at Kulturen. Here, there were rune stones. One, inscribed in red, says, "Ka-ulfr and Autir raised this stone in memory of their brother." I entered the grounds, followed the path to Bosebo church. A poetry reading was being held here. The timbers of the wall behind the altar were painted with Moses holding up the tablets. There was a simple rendition of John the Baptist with the cross. I chose the last pew on the right. On the altar was a figure clad in yellow and blue, an anchor held aloft in her right hand. The poetry dropped from the lips of the readers and clattered to the floor like bits of hacked spruce. As I left I saw two poor boxes dedicated to the support of orphans, the sick, the infirm and those living alone. I emptied my pockets into one of the boxes.

When the editor arrives, I am relieved. I follow him to the canal. A lonely man in a dark suit and dark hat is fishing with a long cane. Beneath the bridge, although it cannot been seen from the street, there is a museum of the old city. Here, the editor says, there are relics of the past from when the city was younger but no kinder. Workers have unearthed an old wall and the stone to which those who had committed unforgivable sins were brought. In this place they were beheaded, burned, broken on a wheel. I make a note to visit this place.

The trip to Sigtuna has a sense of *déjà vu*. If it were not for the roadside signs in Swedish, I tell the editor, I'd be certain I was in Manitoba, returning to see my family. The ditches are filled with the purple spikes of digitalis, tansy and nettle. Sigtuna is the way towns in Sweden used to be, the editor says. Sunlit, tranquil, the old-fashioned buildings lived in by parents and children. We have come to see the ruins of a church. To reach it, we must cross through a graveyard where the rose bushes are brutally pruned in preparation for winter.

I had expected the ruins to be little more than scattered remnants, a few stones covered with grass. Instead, the walls still stand, the stonemason's marks still clear. High up, there are narrow windows. The editor explains that these were for defence against brigands, but no attack ever came. Destruction was the result of neglect and unfaithfulness.

Later, as we stand before a wrought iron globe into which we've set our candles, a guide leading tourists from America declares, "It has no religious significance but people feel they have to do something."

The editor leads me to numerous restaurants. After studying what they have to offer, he rejects them all, decides on Aunt Brown's. A girl with blond braids and an old-fashioned dress with a bow at the back brings coffee and pastry. Seeing the bow, I remember my brother and I, made frantic by the sharp scent of hot gingersnaps, teasing my mother by pulling her apron loose as she baked.

A cat emerges from thick purple flowers at shoulder height, steps daintily onto the table.

III
))) *THE WAITRESS* (((

"I would have told them they couldn't have the cat on the table, but I didn't dare. The foreigner in the raincoat fed it the entire pot of cream. I thought he was going to rub its coat off. Other than that, they hardly said two words to each other. That young couple's still out there under the apple tree. They can't keep their hands off each other. I thought maybe their behaviour had offended the other two. Proper businessmen. Probably up to some deal. Maybe import, export. Plenty of money anyway. Twenty-five hundred crowns for that raincoat. What have they got to look so glum about? Not like me with the rent to pay and never knowing if there'll be enough. Anyway, when I went out, they were gone and they'd left a handsome tip."

IV
))) *THE COOK* (((

The cook, who was worrying about there being enough ham for the evening salads, hadn't noticed the two men or the passionate young couple, but he did take a moment to look out the window. Everyone had gone. The courtyard was empty. A few yellow leaves were scattered over the tables.

Waiting
===

Albert's hands are large, scarred from fish spines and ropes, his knuckles permanently swollen from lifting nets in winter. From first ice until spring breakup, he fishes, even in thirty below, pulling nets from under the ice, warming his hands by dipping his woollen mittens in a pan of hot water.

After breakfast, he caulks his boat. He has winched it ashore, skidding it over a tamarack frame, then, using a pole, levered it onto its gunwales. The wind from the lake is always cold in the morning, so that although the sky is clear and the sun a warm yellow, he wears a parka against the chill. The boat is painted white with a green trim. Built at Riverton, it is sturdy, heavy. But the summer has been hard on it, and now that it is dry, cracks have formed between the boards. He takes a hammer, a chisel and a bag of cotton from the storage shed. Sitting on the stiff grass, he fits a strip of cotton along a crack, presses it into place with the tip of the chisel, then begins to tap it into the crack. It is an easy job but time-consuming. If the children were home, he'd give them the task.

The grass where he has scythed it is stiff, sharp. The ground slopes down to a shingle beach. The beach is made of flat, white pieces of limestone. Beyond this pale band of rock, the lake is smooth, the colour of old tin, without depth or movement. On the horizon there is no land, just sky and water blending together. Only in summer, when heat rises from the lake in waves, does the far shore become visible. Mirages ride above the horizon only to disappear as the air cools.

Since the lake is still, there is no sound except the steady tap

tap of his hammer on the wooden handle of the chisel, the stiff creak of his canvas parka.

He is usually methodical, but today he puts the cotton and tools back before he is finished, turns to the garden. It is smaller than it had once been and needs weeding. Normally, fishermen are not gardeners, and he, himself, when he thinks of it, is surprised by his garden. From eighteen to thirty, he had lived alone, eating out of tin cans, satisfied with rice, instant potatoes, dried fruit, then, while staying in town to be treated for blood poisoning (he had stepped on a gaff and driven it right through his foot), he had met Jane. He had been sitting in the beer parlour with his bad foot up on the seat of a chair. She had known someone at his table and had come to ask for a cigarette. She was young, and he was surprised to see someone like her, pretty, blond, so drunk. She sat down and spent the evening watching them all through half-shut eyes. After that, he seemed to bump into her, in the post office, at the Co-op, at the local café.

At the parlour, he never did more than nurse a beer. She couldn't handle her liquor, gulping it down until her face took on a glazed, angry look. She would sit and stare defiantly at everyone. After a time, she took to sitting beside him and leaving when he left. When he was better and was getting ready to return, she turned up at his boardinghouse with a suitcase and a shopping bag. He didn't know what to say or do, so he didn't say or do anything. When they got to the end of the road and she stepped into his boat, it seemed at once strange and yet perfectly natural.

After she'd been with him eight months, he said to her, "What do you miss the most?" He'd expected her to say the beer parlour or movies or, perhaps, bingo. To his surprise, she'd said fresh fruit and vegetables. He had been taken aback. The end of the road was a day by boat. There was a store there, but it was just one room of a house. The proprietor mostly sold chocolate bars and soft drinks to the Indians. Albert remembered that he'd sometimes seen rather scabby potatoes and some tattered cabbages there. To get to a store with fresh produce was another half-day by car or truck, and the road was only passable if the weather was good.

One day, another fisherman dropped by. He was going to town. Albert asked him to pick up seeds. Albert was rather vague about what he wanted, but he thought that if they managed to grow some onions and a few potatoes, they'd be doing well. When the fisherman stopped again he brought one of everything— zucchini, broccoli, pumpkins, watermelon, muskmelon, tomatoes, strawberry plants, seed potatoes, corn, kohlrabi (Albert had never even heard of kohlrabi). There also were packages of flower seeds. Zinnias, he thought, what am I going to do with zinnias?

But he cut down some trees and used the tractor to pull out the stumps. The soil was rusty red, easy to turn over because there was so much peat moss in it. It was a waste of time, he thought, like planting palm trees in the Arctic, but he kept his mouth shut. They used sticks and lengths of seaming twine to mark rows. He knew nothing would grow, but he used a small motor and some plastic pipe to draw water from the lake. He was amazed when green rows appeared. He hadn't expected them. The morning breeze from the lake was cold, so he built a windbreak from wooden stakes and black plastic garbage bags. He cut out the bottoms of tin cans and set them around the tomato plants and cabbages.

The garden grew. It was like seeing objects fall up instead of down. In the mornings, even before he shaved, he'd look out the screen door just to be sure the plants were really there. He and Jane weeded the garden together. The first thing they ate from it was leaf lettuce and fresh green onions. Potatoes, he thought, I understand potatoes, but sunflower seeds, baby's breath, pansies? They ate fried zucchini, swiss chard, and one day, in fall, Jane sliced open a cantaloupe, revealing its orange flesh. Other fishermen who stopped to visit acted as if the garden wasn't there. Because they couldn't believe it, they refused to acknowledge its existence.

In the fall, they had corn on the cob, tomatoes, fresh potatoes, cabbages. He built a root cellar, ordered glass jars for canning. They fell into the habit of doing the canning together. During the winter, he'd sometimes go into the storeroom just to look at the jars. That winter he did well at fishing, and in the spring, he bought a generator so that they could have electricity. He also bought a freezer.

Jane had their first child, Anne, at the end of the second year.

The year after, she had Paul. Children need good food, she told Albert, and he bought a second freezer. This one was for meat. That fall, he shot a moose. Jane, a meat-cutting diagram beside her, turned it into roasts, stewing meat, steaks and hamburger.

Each winter, they planned the next year's garden, going over the seed catalogues, picking out varieties that might do well during the short, intense summer. They added things. A crabapple tree, raspberry canes, purple cabbage. He built a greenhouse. Jane was able to start seeds in the spring for transplanting.

The year Anne turned six, they didn't know what to do. Neither of them had much education. Albert had dropped out of school after grade nine. Jane had quit in grade ten to go to work as a waitress. They weren't qualified to teach the children at home. That year, they ignored the problem, but when Paul turned six, they got a letter from the Department of Education telling them that their children had to go to school.

I can't live in town, he said. He had never done anything except fish. He knew his area of the lake, every current, every eddy, every reef. He could read the sky, tell from its colour what weather was coming. He could lift nets while his boat rose and fell on waves that would make other men desperately sick. He could go into the bush with a rifle, some lard, flour, beans and rice and stay for two weeks. He didn't need a compass or even a tent. I don't know how, he said.

In September, Jane took the children to town. She rented a two-bedroom house. Every month she got enough money from the fish company to cover her expenses. To help out, she took a job in the parlour waiting on tables. He was to come out at Christmas, but the weather was too bad. His nets froze into the ice and he had all he could do to salvage most of them. They wrote, sending letters back and forth with the freighters who picked up his fish.

After school was out, she and the children came back. He already had the garden prepared. The summer didn't go well. Everything was in too much of a rush. They could stay only six weeks and then had to return to town. Albert and Jane never got over feeling like strangers.

There was no more work in the parlour, so Jane and the children were going to move to Winnipeg. The school would be better. There was more opportunity. A woman she had met had a suite for rent. It was beside a community centre that had a swimming pool and skating rink. Paul wanted to play peewee hockey and Anne was going to take figure skating. Albert didn't know what to say. Living on his own all winter had made it harder to talk about things.

The second summer, Paul had a bad case of measles and was quite sick. Afterward, there were complications. Anne didn't want to leave because she was taking painting in the park. Albert went to Winnipeg. All the time he was there, he was restless. There was nothing to do. The kids were in classes and Jane was at work all day. There was no real yard, just a patch of gravel and mud beside the garage. He tried planting a garden there. A few things started to come up, but then someone backed in to turn around and drove over the plants. He went for walks, but all the time he was going through Eaton's or the Bay, he knew he should be getting ready for fall fishing. There were nets to be spread and boxed. He had to get bridles ready. Now that he had only himself to feed, the garden was much too large. He went back at the end of July.

At Christmas, Jane sent him a card and a pair of socks. He'd sent Paul an ermine skin and Anne a birch bark doll cradle. He had not been able to think of anything for Jane. Finally, he made her a bouquet of dried flowers from the garden. At the end of May, she sent a message saying they'd come on July first. Later, a note came saying she'd got a new job and so wouldn't have any holidays. She said she hoped the garden was doing well.

He wanted to write to her, to tell her there had been a late frost, then a swarm of grasshoppers. He wanted to ask for her advice on keeping out snails, to tell her about the morning a bear had picked the strawberry plants clean, but he didn't have the words for it.

The Cave

===

I first came upon Sigga Anderson at her cousin's farm. I had knocked on the screen door and got no reply, so I went around to the back and there, wearing a wide-brimmed hat, a white dress and no shoes, she was picking raspberries. I must have made some slight sound, for she glanced up.

Her blond hair was curled to her shoulders. Her skin was damp and pink with the heat and her lips were red with the juice of the berries she had eaten. We stared at each other without saying anything, then she rose and held the white enamel bowl toward me. The berries were piled so high that some cascaded down and dropped to the ground.

"*Godan daginn*," she said.

"*Godan daginn*," I said.

"*Tala thu Islenzku?*"

"*Nay*," I replied.

"That's too bad," she said, in the slightly ponderous way that Icelanders have of speaking English. "You are Valgardson. I recognize you from Einar's description."

"Is Einar home?"

"They've all gone to the beach."

"But not you."

"Would you have me roasted alive? I'm not used to the sun yet."

"And the mosquitoes?"

"They're devils."

She put the white basin into my hand and lifted up her dress for me to look. Her legs were spotted with angry-looking lumps. Iceland does not have mosquitoes, and Icelanders who come to Canada suffer terrible reactions when they are first stung.

"Has Einar any beer in the well?" I asked. She let down her dress. "It was a long ride on my bicycle."

She was, I discovered, twenty, single and quick-tempered. The last did not keep me from making daily trips to Einar's. Nor was I deterred by the fact she was Gunnar Thordarson's great-granddaughter.

We went walking in the hayfields together and along the edge of the poplar bush, picking wild roses and Indian paintbrush and wild lilies. We filled buckets with berries.

More and more often, though, our trips ended at one of Einar's haystacks. At mealtimes and in the evenings, there were good-natured comments around the table about the work it took to make a good stack and how, if the tops were thrown about, the hay would not survive the rain and snow.

Until then I had not even considered marriage. As a matter of fact, I had frequently bragged that I would not marry until I was thirty and well established. Since I still had three years to go, my relationship with Sigga caused some sly comments and smiles.

By late August, I no longer cared about looking foolish. Quite confidently, I asked her to marry me. I didn't go down on bended knee. It would have been quite impractical. We had just made love and were lying on top of one of Einar's precious haystacks. It is one of those special times I remember with painful clarity.

There were three small, fluffy clouds sliding slowly westward. There was no sound except for the occasional shifting in the hay. I was lying with one arm under my head, the other around Sigga.

If I remember the incident as clearly as I think I do, I said, "If you wanted, we could get married before school starts."

"No." She said it so quietly and agreeably that, at first, I took it for assent. When it finally registered that I had been refused, I rolled toward her to look into her pale green eyes.

"Sooner?"

"Not sooner. Not later."

I felt as though my heart had stopped. I would have been angry except that I was so taken aback. "But I love you," I protested.

"Yes," she agreed.

"And you love me?"

"Yes."

With that, my heart started to beat again. Or, at least, I became aware that it was still working.

"Then why in heaven's name..." I had been so sure of her reply that I had already rented a small log cabin behind the school. It had a kitchen, living room and two small bedrooms. There were red shutters on the windows and a natural stone chimney. It had taken all my persuasiveness to convince the owner, who lived in Winnipeg and used it for a summer cottage, to let me have it from September until the end of June. "I've rented Brynolver's cabin," I blurted out.

"Good. Living there with you will be nice."

"Then, for God's sake, let's get married."

She let her eyes slide away from mine. "No. I would like to live with you, but I won't marry."

"Are you crazy?"

It was not a good thing to say. I felt her stiffen. I had momentarily forgotten that her great-grandfather had been Gunnar Thordarson and that her father was Valdi Anderson.

There are times to be silent. I lay back and studied the pale blue sky. Normally, Sigga would have curled against my side but now, although she remained with her head on my arm, her body was stiff.

"Remember the roses," I said.

One day after she had fallen asleep, I slid down the haystack, ran to the side of the road, and using my shirt like a sack, filled it with the petals of wild roses. I returned, scattered them over her naked, golden body. When she awoke and sat up, rose petals filled her lap, clung to her hair. We made love again and the bruised petals engulfed us in their sweet scent.

"If I marry, my husband will want sons. I will have no sons."

Earlier, the thought that I had a rival had made my head ring with jealousy. Now, I suddenly wished it were that simple.

"I'm a high school teacher. If we live together, the board will have fits."

"I had promised myself to care for no one," she answered quietly. "Then you appeared with your one pant leg held in place with a bicycle clip."

"I had promised not to marry until I was thirty and then only to a widow with a good income."

"It was your beard and the shocked look in your eyes." She squeezed my hand.

"This is madness," I answered.

"If only it weren't," she answered and began to cry.

If this were a piece of fiction, all this description would be irrelevant detail. I would follow Poe's dictum and start closer to the climax. I would organize it toward one effect and ruthlessly eliminate everything else. But it is not fiction. What matters is not plot or theme but only that you understand. To ask, for example, "What is your motive?" of someone is to imply a simplicity about life that, except for the stupidest of people, is hopelessly inaccurate.

What was my motive in researching the lives of Sigga's great-grandfather and father? To prove that they were not crazy? To reassure Sigga that if she was to have a son, he would escape their fate? To reassure myself of the same thing? To defuse the innuendo and gossip that have persisted about this family for over seventy years? And more. Some of which I, myself, am still not clear about.

Life, unfortunately, is not as tractable as fiction. I cannot invent my characters or their lives. They already exist. I can only attempt to discover and understand.

I began by visiting people I knew. There was nothing formal about it, nothing, at first, even deliberate. I'd drop by for coffee and, after we were settled around the kitchen table, ask questions about Gunnar and Valdi.

It was unproductive. Not so much because everyone was deliberately evasive, but because each person had such small fragments of Gunnar and Valdi's lives. At times, I felt like I was collecting the parts of a shattered stained glass window, the pieces of which had been picked up by people over the years and tucked away in drawers or cupboards. Some had forgotten where they put them, others still knew where they were and, if I was lucky, would go get them to give to me. Some, because of the passage of time, had mixed them up with pieces of glass from other windows and gave me fragments that caused nothing but confusion. Some pieces were never picked up and were irretrievably lost.

If it was not for the fact that Sigga discovered and gave me a fish box full of Gunnar's diaries and letters, plus her father's correspondence, I would have given up. These records were not complete. However, to stick to my stained glass analogy, these records provided the lead in the window.

Because I'm a short story writer—W. D. Valgardson is hardly a name to conjure with, but here and there, people have read my stories—I'm very conscious that if this were fiction, I'd not begin like this, with a lot of explanation and excuse making. Instead, I'd go right to the heart of the story and I'd leave myself out of it, become an effaced narrator, or if I used the first person, it would not really be me, but a mask.

One of the first things you learn in telling a story is to condense time for dramatic effect, but how can I condense four generations? In a piece of fiction, I cast about for the right structure, the method of telling the story that will get me closest to the truth. This research and retelling in which I have been involved has nearly driven me to distraction because there is no structure except the one that life has imposed, and if there is any lesson about life, it escapes me. What I have finally resolved to do is to take the coward's way out—tell the story in a reasonably chronological fashion.

My beginning is arbitrary. I chose it because there is a major change in the lives of the main participants, but I could equally as well have begun elsewhere. In life there are no real beginnings or endings. There are so many moments where one can say, "That's where it started," and, in most cases, it is both true and false. Life is nothing if not untidy.

))) GUNNAR AND RUNA (((

Gunnar's family owned a good-sized farm, Hagar,[1] but the volcanic eruptions of 1875 reduced it to half its size. Just before the

---

1. Icelandic word for meadow. Icelandic farms were all named. The tradition was so strong it was carried to Canada.

eruption, Gunnar had married Helga Jonsdottir. The marriage, by all accounts, was an unhappy one. Both were quick-tempered and proud. They took offence easily and were slow to give up grudges. Helga's father was, in Icelandic terms, well-to-do, and one day, when Gunnar—his family nearly reduced to penury by the destruction of their land—refused Helga something she wanted, she said she would ask her father for it. Enraged, he slapped her. She picked up a knife and, if being six months pregnant had not made her awkward, would have killed him. Instead, she left him with a cut that ran from his eye to his jaw. Sometime during the next week, with the help of a farmhand, she returned to her father's house.

Gunnar followed her and tried to force her to return home with him. Her relatives stopped him. He began to drink heavily and, at every opportunity, to abuse his wife's family with scathing verses that he recited to anyone who would listen. Then, abruptly, after his wife gave birth, Gunnar's behaviour changed. He called on her—sober, repentant, his voice gentle—gave her silver equal to the price of a cow. He no longer tried to get his wife back, but from time to time, he visited Reykjavik to see his daughter and to leave *skyr*[2] and mutton. Because of what had occurred, he would not enter his in-laws' house. Instead, he and Helga walked with the child to the home of mutual friends. This went on for two years.

Then, abruptly, Gunnar sold his farm and notified his wife that he intended to give the child part of the money from the sale. He also told her he was emigrating to North America. Two days before he was to leave, he arrived at his in-laws' front door and asked his wife if he might spend some time alone with the child. It was unlikely, as he pointed out, that he would ever see her again.

His behaviour had been so exemplary that Helga agreed. Besides, Gunnar's ship was not due to arrive for another day. They were gone all afternoon, but Helga was not overly concerned. She expected that Gunnar was going from house to house saying

---

2. An Icelandic yogurt.

goodbye to his friends. However, when supper time came and passed, she began to worry. She put on her coat and went to see if she could find them.

It was too late. Gunnar and Runa were already on their way to Denmark on a small freighter. His planning was meticulous and must have been started shortly after his daughter was born.

))) GUNNAR AND RUNA IN WINNIPEG (((

Gunnar and Runa arrived in Halifax on July 23, 1878. They travelled from there to Toronto, stayed in Toronto three months and arrived in Winnipeg on October 28. Egil Fjelsted was a child at the time. He went with his father to the CPR station to meet them. He was very young and did not actually remember their arrival, but afterward he heard about it so often that he said it was as if he remembered it.[3]

October was no time to be arriving in Winnipeg. Summer construction and farm work were over. Gunnar spoke hardly any English, so most nonlabouring jobs were closed to him. He and Runa boarded in the West End at the Fjelsteds' until Crooked Eye Oddleifson turned up.

Oddleifson was a barrel of a man, slope-shouldered, with big, shovel-like hands and one eye that turned in so much he appeared to be looking at his own nose. He hired Gunnar to help him with fishing. No one else would go. Oddleifson's camp was more isolated than most. He had a reputation for feeding his help poorly, working them hard and, if he could get away with it, not paying their wages. That Gunnar accepted the job indicated how desperate he was becoming.

He could not take Runa. Even if she could survive the hundred and fifty—mile trek in the cold, the camp was no place for a child. The two men would leave every day before dawn and stay on the ice until dark. Reluctantly, he agreed to leave her in Mrs. Fjelsted's care.

---

3. Fjelsted, Egil. Died, Betel, Gimli, Manitoba, 1968.

))) *GUNNAR AND ODDLEIFSON* (((

The weather was bitter. Ten degrees below zero during the day. Thirty below at night. Oddleifson had brought a horse and sleigh but used it only for supplies. To keep warm, they walked. Fort Garry, Gimli, Icelandic River, Mikley and, finally, all the way to the camp. They slept at stopping places along the way. Breakfast they got from the owners of the houses, but lunch and supper were bread and smoked fish they kept inside their jackets so it wouldn't freeze.

It must have been a frightening experience for a man like Gunnar, who, in Iceland, was used to staying close to his own farm. Day after day, he walked over endless miles of drifted snow. In his diary, he compares it to entering a white hell. Before they reached the camp, he became snow-blind, and Oddleifson had to tie a rope around his waist and attach it to the sleigh. Gunnar was forced to follow helplessly, sometimes walking, sometimes running, frequently falling, while, behind him, the known world retreated.

The camp was worse than he expected. It was one room carelessly kept. Life in a fish camp was hard enough, but Oddleifson was dirty without need. What he could have done to make life more bearable, he did not do.

The two men did not get along well. Oddleifson had been described by others as insensitive, even brutal. Because of his eye, he had a strange way of turning his head to one side and hunching his shoulders. It earned him a second nickname of "the Bull."

Gunnar, besides being a farmer, had been a poet of some reputation. Moreover, he was well educated and sensitive. Having to live day in and day out with Oddleifson, with his gross habits and crude conversation, must have been difficult. How it would have worked out was never discovered, because three months after they began fishing together, Crooked Eye put an ice chisel through his foot. His uncleanliness did him in. The wound infected, and within a week, he died.

Now, do you see what is so maddening? It is as if everything is connected and yet nothing is connected. Do you know what I mean? If this were a piece of fiction, I could have foreshadowed, dramatized and then subtly not revealed what actually happened. You would have deduced that Gunnar, isolated, angered, actually killed Oddleifson. There would be an epiphany and you and I would share a secret understanding of men's hearts.

I can do no such thing. I can find no evidence that Gunnar stuck an ice chisel through Oddleifson's foot, rubbed it with horse shit and then waited for him to die.

Nor can I make anything of the fact Gunnar did not go for help. Given the distance and the weather, there was no point in trying to take Oddleifson in on the sleigh, even if he had permitted it. What Gunnar did do, once Oddleifson was dead, was haul his body onto the roof of the shed so that the animals could not get at it, then each day, as his work permitted, chiselled frozen ground until he had a grave.

At this point, Gunnar was faced with a choice. He could return to Winnipeg and a winter's unemployment or he could stay by himself in the camp. He had received no payment for his work and, if anything, was worse off than he had been before. He chose to stay.

Although he did not realize it, the pattern of his life was set.[4] He lived in the camp and fished fall and winter. July he spent with Runa at the Fjelsteds'. A number of times, as Runa grew older, he talked of having her come and live with him, but Mrs. Fjelsted would not hear of it.

During his second year in the camp, he decided something that, at the time, seemed of no significance, and yet it ultimately affected him more than anything else he had done. His problem and his attempt to solve it was this.

During the winter, he kept his perishable food on the roof. Once the spring thaw set in, however, he had no way of keeping food fresh.

He began to search the limestone cliffs along the lake for a cave. What he hoped to find was one deep enough that if it was

---

4. There was an attempt some years later by a cousin of Oddleifson's to claim the camp as an inheritance. However, he was in Iceland, and Lake Winnipeg was a great distance away. When Gunnar heard of the claim, he only replied, "Let him come and get it."

packed with ice and snow, would keep food frozen through the warm months. He searched for days and was on the point of giving up when he found what he was looking for—but in a most extraordinary way.

Along with being a poet, he had always been something of a mystic. Perhaps that's why events took the turn they did. He became ill, suffered nightmares and existed, for a time, in that half-asleep, half-awake mixture of reality and fantasy that leaves one uncertain of one's own sanity, for in it the familiar world shifts and changes into a quicksand of images. Finally, the fever broke and he slept soundly. During this sleep, he had a dream, and in this dream, he claims he found the entrance to the cave. The cliff appeared before him in great detail, as though it were magnified. He scrutinized the cliff, checking and rechecking all the cracks, then stopped before a place where the rock was thick with moss. There seemed to be nothing of interest there, but then the moss darkened and the rocks slanted inward.

When he woke, he remembered the dream clearly. However, he was still weak with fever and did not go out for another three days. Each night, as if it had a life of its own, the dream returned. When, at last, he was well enough to go out, the first thing he did was row a boat along the lake shore to the spot where the dream had taken him. When he came to a section of rock of which he had dreamt, it was as he remembered it. In the dream, as he had reached out to pull away the moss, he had always awakened, but now there was no waking. He felt the moss thick and moist under his fingertips; felt it tear in a long sheet. Here was a fissure that was just big enough for him to enter by angling his shoulders sideways.

He first thought it only a crack, but then, it widened. The air was cold. He went back to the beach, found a long strip of birch bark, set it afire and, using it like a torch, explored the narrow cave. Five feet from the entrance, the floor was a solid slab of ice. Where there were cracks in the ceiling, icicles hung down like stalactites. He was so excited by his discovery that in his diary, he exclaims, "What a find! Now, I can keep food all year if I wish."[5]

---

5. July 6, 1879.

During the next winter, his only visitors were freighters who came to load his fish. He did not mind. He had brought with him a small library, and although most of his money went for Runa's support, he bought philosophical books that dealt, in one way or the other, with the existence of reality.

None fascinated him more than the theory of Bjorn Bjornson,[6] who claimed the soul never slept but inhabited bodies in two worlds and passed back and forth between them. What we call madness was not, according to this theorist, the inability to tell what was real and what was hallucination but a leakage of information from one existence to another.

There is very little description of Gunnar's appearance and no photograph. We know that toward the end of 1910 he grew a full beard. His grey hair he let grow until it reached his shoulders. He wore a beaded deerhide jacket, which he had bought from the Indians. That is known because Axel Arnason, the freighter, recorded this in a report to his sister in a letter.[7]

At first, the cave was no more than a convenience, a place to keep deer and moose meat and enough fish to supply his huskies during the spring and fall when he could not get on the water. It was only later that it became an obsession.

During the winter of 1914, Axel Arnason arrived to pick up fish. There was no one in the cabin. That, in itself, meant nothing. Gunnar could be on the lake or in the bush. Axel lit the fire and waited. No one came, and as he said in his deposition to the police,[8] after a time he became nervous. The sleigh was outside the door, but there was no sign of the dogs. There were no tracks in the snow and there had been a heavy snowfall a week before.

He went outside, kicked at a mound of snow and found a dead husky. Then another and another, all still chained to their ground pegs. In the lean-to, the horse had frozen to death standing up.

It took the police a month to get a man out to the camp. There was no rush. Gunnar was certainly dead, probably under the ice

6. Bjornson, Bjorn, 1750–1797, *Souls Adrift*, Oslo, private printing, 57 pp.
7. Icelandic collection, University of Manitoba.
8. RCMP archives, Regina, Saskatchewan.

or frozen in a snowdrift. His belongings were collected and put in fish boxes and shipped to Runa.

Gunnar's Diary
—translated by Miss S. Stephanson

August 18, 1911
The cave is seventy-five feet long, ten feet high at its highest point and four feet across. Its general shape is that of a canoe with blunt ends.

August 19, 1911
I returned to the cave today. This time I took a better torch, which I fashioned from reeds and pitch. The walls are thick with the past. It is like memory frozen in stone. Animals and plants bleached white. I made some sketches.

His diary, more and more, records the details of the cave. He made a grid of string so that floor, walls, roof, were divided into three-inch squares. Each segment he mapped. At the same time, his recording of weather, of nets, of fish, begins to fall off.

Gradually, intertwined with his studies, grew the thesis for his essay "The Seasons and the Blood." From his reading, he began to collect every example that would prove history is cyclical and that the future can be predicted from the past. In 1939, Runa discovered this essay, made a copy and offered it to a number of Scandinavian publishers; however, arriving as it did in the face of a rapidly advancing technological age whose justification for its excesses lay in the assumption that time is linear and all change leads to improvement, it was rejected.

September 20, 1911
Today, I smashed through the curtain of ice at the rear of the cave. My axe discovered a narrow slit in the rock that I could hardly squeeze through. What is there?

What was there, he discovered, was a series of caves, a labyrinthine honeycomb that underlay the entire area. The surface looked, from above, impervious, solid, real, but although it supported infinite trees, marshes and animals, its solidity was only illusion. It was a secret world discovered by dreams, a secret world that altered his whole concept of reality.

For a time, he was satisfied to do no more than recalculate his earlier findings, refining and rechecking his measurements of the antechamber. On sheets of brown wrapping paper, he sketched each fossil in detail. He began to keep track of the waxing and waning of the ice. He planned to order finely calibrated instruments so that he could measure the annual lengthening of the stalactites.

The new entrance became a torment, a question demanding an answer. In December 1911, he was determined to block this entrance with stone. A week later, he was equally determined to squeeze through with a torch and a rope. In March he had still not committed himself, but he recorded that he had had a series of nightmares, all to do with his vacillation. Finally, at the end of May, forced into idleness by a spring thaw, he gathered five hundred feet of string, a hundred feet of stout rope, a lantern, four pitons made from ring bolts and a hand axe. He also took a dozen matches, a pound of mixed raisins and two *hardfisk*.

He drove a piton into a crevice close to the entrance, fastened the string to it, then forced his way into a small cavern that led downward to a larger cavern, which he described as big as the biggest whale.

The diary for the next two years is missing, but a letter to this daughter dated January 1914 stated that he had explored numerous caves, each one unique and full of wonders. In one there was a pool, and from it, he caught blind fish. He added that he was afraid but that he could not stop. "As much as I have learned the secrets of the earth," he said, "I have learned more about myself."

On the table the day Axel the freighter discovered the empty cabin, the dead dogs and horse, was this cryptic note:

"*To the farthest depth . . .*"

))) *R U N A* (((

By the time Gunnar had disappeared, Runa was married and had a son called Valdi. For some years, Gunnar had not come to town.

The only communication between him and Runa were his infrequent letters. The result was that when he disappeared he was little missed. The few times he had visited his daughter, he had spent most of his time in his room sitting at the window and smoking his pipe. Silence had become a habit with him. Over the years the Fjelsteds had become Runa's true family.

The boxes of Gunnar's belongings were stored in the attic of Runa's Sargeant Avenue house. There they would have stayed if it had not been for Valdi.

))) *VALDI ANDERSON* (((

Runa's son became a teacher and taught for a year at Hecla.

It was there that, for the first time, he heard the Fjelsteds were not his blood relatives. The shock was so great that, for a time, he refused to believe what he had been told. At last, on a weekend trip to Winnipeg, he confronted his mother, who reluctantly admitted that his grandfather had been Gunnar. When he pressed her, she refused to talk about it.

"Leave it," she cried. "You did not know him. I did not know him. What does it matter?"

"It matters."

"The Fjelsteds loved me."

"What was he like?"

"I don't know."

He was still young and filled with the anger that seethes within the young like unexplained fire. He began to shout.

"Are you ashamed of him?"

"No. It's not that."

"Then what?"

"He lived. He died. I hardly saw him."

"How did he die?"

"I don't know." Runa, who was unused to confrontation, began to wring her hands. Her own early sense of abandonment, her own fears, welled up like debris that had been hidden beneath the waters of a deep lake and suddenly stirred. "Nobody knows."

Like his maternal grandfather, Valdi was large. Like him, too, he could take offence easily and nurse a grudge.

His mother, desperate to stop the questions, thought of the boxes under the eaves. She offered him these in return for peace.

There were three wooden fish boxes filled with letters, books, drawings and diaries. Valdi impatiently pulled loose the lids, certain that what had been hidden would now be revealed.

"I can't read this," he said.

Everything was in Icelandic.

In spite of this defeat, he took the boxes with him. Perhaps he was afraid that his mother would burn the contents, then deny their existence. From time to time, he returned to the boxes, puzzling over the carefully executed drawings of trilobites, clam shells, a feathery leaf. The books and diaries were dry and brittle, the paper yellow, the letters as fragile as last fall's leaves.

Caught up in the rush of teaching and marriage, he was too busy to pay much attention to these relics, but still, they posed a question. It was not the kind of question that demanded an answer but the kind that nagged, the way the picture of a small, ragged child begging will nag at the conscience of the well fed.

Do you see what I mean about this task? God help me. What love will drive a man to do. There are too many characters. Everybody gets involved. Already we've got four generations. Gunnar—Runa—Valdi—Sigga. Why can I not just condense it, make it less messy? There is no unity of time or place. Aristotle, wherever you are, give God some good advice. Tell Him to get organized.

Here's Valdi so busy teaching classes, grading papers, screwing his pretty little wife from Akureyri, taking classes for his certificate, repairing the roof, that he sets aside these three bloody boxes and, now and again, late at night, looks them over, promising himself that when he gets time, he'll learn to read and write Icelandic and translate them. I keep wanting to shout "Action. Get on with it. To hell with the picnic. To hell with going to Gimli for *Islindingadagurinn*. Never mind that damn birthday party."

Five years passed. How's that for a transition? Bugger the details, the character development, go for the main point. Five years passed, and damned if he didn't start to take Icelandic lessons in 1944 when he got a job teaching in Winnipeg at Kelvin High School. Twice a week, he took lessons with Rev. V. J. Eylands, D.D.[9] At last—in spite of the protests of his wife, who wanted him to get rid of the papers—little by little, he began to translate.

The more he read, the more the idea of the cave took hold. He began to question every elderly person he came across who might know some part of his grandfather's story. Soon he began to seek these people out. He followed rumours. He wrote letters.

He began to dream about the cave. From the notes and diagrams, he knew it more intimately than his own house. Awake, he found it intruding upon his thoughts. When he was certain he had pinpointed the location of the cabin, he bought a boat.

On a weekend at the end of July, he drove to Pine Dock. The road began in pavement, changed to gravel and finally dwindled to one lane of mud. Beside a sagging dock, an old woman lived in an abandoned ice shed. He saw her face behind a dusty window, but she refused to answer his knock. A black goat was tethered to a tree stump. He slept in his car. Before dawn, he slid his boat into the dark water. He travelled slowly, staying close to the shore and keeping the map on his knee. The forest pressed to the very edge of the lake. When he reached his destination and shut off his motor, the silence amazed him.

He was rewarded with the remains of a log cabin. The roof had collapsed and rotted away, but the silvered walls were still standing. Grass grew thickly from the mud floor. Outside the walls, grass and moose maple filled what had been a clearing. He could, when he closed his eyes, see the ice-covered window, the frozen dogs, the snow drifting in ragged lines over the ground. He returned the next weekend with his wife and daughter. He cleared a twenty-foot circle around the cabin. The discovery of the rusted remains of the metal pegs that had held the dogs excited him.

He did not have to teach until September, so he returned to Winnipeg, bought enough supplies to last him a month and returned by himself. Because of the cold wind off the lake, he set

---

9. Dr. Valdimar J. Eylands, an able preacher and writer. A leader in the Icelandic community.

up his tent inside the cabin walls. A day after he arrived, he began his search. For all the details in the diary about the cave itself, the precise location was never described.

The shoreline was in ruins. Great columns of limestone had been weathered from the cliffs. Trees grew in profusion. He was not discouraged. He knew that the entrance could not be far away. A half-mile in either direction was the outside limit. A greater distance would have made transporting supplies difficult.

Clambering over the rocks was strenuous. At first, he had to rest frequently. As the days passed, he grew stronger and was able to search for hours on end. He took three rolls of film. He also had collected all the information about the area that he could find. It did not surprise him that there was no mention of caves. Knowledge, he had discovered during his academic career, looked extensive only until a specific answer was sought.

In the middle of August, he found a number of false leads, caves that disappointed him by going only a short distance before stopping. On August 25, he found a cave he thought was the one for which he was looking. On August 26, measurements demonstrated that it was not the right cave. When he was ready to give up, he found, in his grandfather's dreams, the clue he needed.

He closed his eyes and constructed for himself the cliffs as he remembered them. When he returned to the cliffs, he realized his memory had been inaccurate. Rather than continue his earlier fruitless physical search, he sat just offshore in his boat and watched the cliffs until he was certain their image was printed on his mind. Twice more he had to return, but then he lay on the grass before the log cabin and slept. In his sleep, he saw the entire cliff in every detail. A purple shadow and the slant of some rocks told him what he needed to know.

On August 30, he used a crowbar to clear the entrance. The cave was not as long as it had been, but he knew immediately that he was in the right place. His grandfather's piton he found embedded in ice.

He played his light over the entrance to the deeper caves. The walls were all highlights and shadows. Ahead was darkness and the unknown. Overwhelmed by his fear of being lost in the maze that he knew stretched before him, he resolved to return home and burn his grandfather's materials.

The next morning, he changed his mind. Instead of starting south, he entered the cave. He took with him fifteen hundred feet of blue thread to unroll as he went. The time of his leaving is known, for he wrote it down to the minute: 6:15, August 31.

Six months later, his wife returned to Iceland with Sigga. There Sigga stayed until just before we met at Einar's farm and had our summer together.

Because of her refusal to marry me, because of who we were, because of the times, our relationship did not last. I searched, during this time we had together, God help me, I searched, trying to find answers so that she need have no fears, but I could not then and cannot now make any sense out of it. No epiphany. Not for me. Not for you.

Sigga left. One day I went to work. When I came back, she was gone. A year after, I heard that she was living in Iceland. I wrote again and again but never received a reply.

I married someone else. That didn't work out either. We're separated and waiting for a divorce. I doubt if being married to anyone would have worked out. Sigga was too much in my heart. That summer we had together, drenched in passion and colour, made everyone and everything seem pale by comparison. Still, as the years passed, even Sigga faded.

Then a week ago, a letter arrived. It was from a Ragnar Williamson. He is, he says, my son. Sigga, he informs me, is dead. Cancer.

His mother was pregnant when she left here. She returned to Iceland, bore him, raised him, never married, never told him who his father was. Now, with a great deal of effort, he has tracked me down.

He is coming to visit me. He wants, above all, to learn about his family.

The Man from Snaefellsness

===

"*Tala thu Islenzku?*" she asked.

"What?" I said, staring at the phone. I didn't remember picking it up.

"Do you speak Icelandic?"

"Who wants to know? Good God, it's four in the morning."

"Is this Axel Borgfjord? I'm calling on behalf of the Committee for Relationships with Canada."

"Who are you?"

"Axel, who is it?" Helen mumbled. Her face was still in her pillow and her voice was muffled, softened with sleep.

The telephone crackled with static, and the faint woman's voice added, "We would like you to visit Iceland as our guest. Have you been to Iceland?"

"Is it the babysitter?" When Helen stayed overnight, I paid for a sitter. Three of the four last times, her daughter had managed to get sick.

"No. It's a prank."

"I'm sorry, I didn't hear you," the voice said.

"What do you want me to do? Write an article?" I asked, playing along. I have some peculiar friends. As kids they used to phone up corner stores and ask if the store had Prince Albert in a tin, and when the owner said yes, they'd shriek with delight and say, "Then let him out." Now their gags are more sophisticated, more complex, but their sense of humour just as juvenile.

"You do nothing. We know all about your writing. Your stories and plays. Now we want you learn about us."

"If everything is paid for. Sure, I'll come."

"Yes. You pay nothing. We will take you to the farm from which your great-grandfather came."

"What do you know about my great-grandfather?" I snapped, but simultaneously she said, "I'll send you the ticket. *Godan daginn,*" and the phone went dead and I shouted, "Wait, I can't come. Don't..." and then I stopped and sat staring at the phone. Sitting in the darkness, it was as though I could hear the distant surf of Iceland breaking on the skerries, shattering on the shingle beach my great-grandfather had described to me. The ice grinding itself to pieces at the foot of the home field.

I fell asleep to dream of hills. At first I thought I was alone, then, in the distance, against the horizon, a viking with a spear, then closer, on another hill, another viking, then another. I would have fled, but suddenly, appearing out of deep fissures in the lava behind me, looking like my father and grandfather, my brother and uncles, came other men, their weapons drawn, facing those who now thronged from the hills. One of those who confronted me raised his axe, and I shouted and struck out with my sword and battle was joined. My kinsmen and I fought un-ceasingly, but no matter how many we killed, there were always more. And then it was morning and the apple tree outside my window was drenched in bloom, and I reached out and plucked a sprig of blossoms and gave them to Helen. I wondered if I had only dreamt the phone call like I had dreamt the battle.

"No, you were quite rude to her. By the end you were shout-ing," Helen said over coffee.

The battle faded away and I'd nearly forgotten about the phone call until two weeks later when an airplane ticket arrived by registered mail.

"I thought you were going to tell them you couldn't come?" Helen said. She was helping me plant the garden.

"I forgot about it."

"It's for August first. A charter out of Winnipeg."

"I can't go. Anyway, why should I? Good God, my great-grandfather arrived in Sandy Bar in 1878. No one has ever gone back. It's history."

"Talk Icelandic to me," Helen said.

"Forget it."

"Come on," she answered, holding up some marigolds. "How

does an Icelander say 'Let's hop in the sack'?"

"I haven't the faintest idea."

"Everybody can swear in their mother tongue."

"English is my mother tongue. I was born here."

"How do you say 'grandma'?"

"Let's drop it, okay?"

"Boy, are you touchy," she said, her feelings hurt. She was vaguely WASP, but not in any connected way, no accent, no relatives in the British Isles, no Christmas customs except frantic shopping and paying too much for a tree imported from the U.S. She missed what I had, she said, belonging to a specific place. She loved going to the Multicultural Festival and drifting from booth to booth, eating *langosh, satay, peroghis*, and washing it all down with cappuccino and German beer. The folk dance costume she wore to parties was made up of pieces from India, Yugoslavia, Germany, Finland. People who didn't know better thought it was authentic.

"*Amma*," I offered. Her white blouse showed the tanned curve of her neck and a loop of dark hair had fallen over one eye. I reached up and brushed her hair back over her ear. Although she was thirty, there was something innocent about her. When she played about the yard with her daughter, it was like both of them were four. "That's how you say 'grandma.' "

We had planned a romantic afternoon together. The wine was in the fridge and the avocado and shrimp prepared for lunch, but the glow was off the day. I threw the ticket into a dresser and slammed the drawer shut.

What was Iceland to me? I was fourth-generation Canadian. That should have been the end of the matter, but every time I went out to cut the grass or weed the garden or trim the ivy, my great-grandfather's face appeared. At times, I could smell his pipe tobacco. More than once I was certain he was standing behind me, watching, and I turned suddenly as if to catch him but there was never anyone there. At last, I gave up. Come on, I said out loud, let's get this over with, and suddenly, it was like I was six again, dressed in my sailor's uniform, standing in my great-grandfather's back yard. He was wearing his black pants, suspenders and his long underwear but no shirt. He was splitting wood, and as he chopped, he and my father were talking.

"Are you going to come to *Islindingadagurinn* this year?" my father asked.

"Those who enjoy these things can go."

"All your friends will be there."

"If Einar from Vithir is still alive, or Hannes from Arborg, they know where to find my house." All the time they talked, he split kindling from a round of birch.

"The Ladies Aid is serving coffee and rosettes. Fresh whipped cream."

"*Hreppsomagur* don't go to celebrations." When he was fourteen, he had been given a one-way ticket to Canada. Five dollars in his pocket. He knew no English. During the trip eleven people had died. He had stolen a language text from one of the dead women. After that, when he had needed something, he pointed to a word in Icelandic and people would read the word beside it in English. Then they would point to a word in English and he'd read the Icelandic. "Let them choke on their rosettes and whipped cream."

"That was sixty-seven years ago."

"Do you know what they wrote in the paper after they kicked people like me out? They wrote that when times got tough, we were cowards and ran away. I think maybe they got it backwards. Pontius Pilate didn't die. He just moved to Iceland and had lots of children."

Stiff-necked, unforgiving, proud, Icelandic to the core. That was Ketil, my great-grandfather. At one time, his father had been *bondi*, a farmer, and his mother had been *husmothir*. They operated an independent farm, which they rented from the church. A volcanic eruption covered most of the hayfields with ash, and toxic gases poisoned the cattle so that their legs became disjointed and tumours grew on their bones. Rather than see them die in agony, Ketil and his father had slaughtered both cattle and sheep with an axe. To try to feed themselves and the five others still on the farm, they turned to the sea. They had an open boat suitable for four men. Each day, the two of them with their two hired men risked the surf, then rowed three miles to fish for cod. They might have survived, but the weather turned unseasonably cold, filling the bay with ice. They were reduced to scavenging along the beach for fish that were washed up in the ice. The women gathered lichens to make porridge.

When there was nothing but starvation, Ketil's father, along with his family, was forced by law to return to the Snaefellsness Peninsula, to the *hreppar*, or district, where he was born. That made them *hreppsomagur*, beggarmen, welfare cases. Ketil's father pleaded with the district council to let the family remain together. He was prepared to fix up an abandoned house, but the local farmers needed hired help. They insisted that the family be broken up, each going to work for a different farmer. The local council went further and got an order to seize everything except the clothes that the three of them were wearing. When Ketil's father protested, he was told that poor men who could not look after their families did not need more than one set of clothes. They were worked from dawn to dusk, but the farmer responsible for Ketil, rather than face years of feeding him, paid his passage to Canada. Ketil had tried to resist, but two burly farmers had forcibly put him on a Danish fishing boat. Two weeks later he was in Scotland. Three weeks after that he was in Montreal. Once there was no hope of turning back, Ketil could think of only one destination. *Nya Island.* New Iceland.

It took him six months, but finally, he reached Winnipeg, and with wages he had earned as a labourer, purchased a ticket on a freight boat that was going to Icelandic River.

He stood on the narrow deck as the boat entered Lake Winnipeg. By this time he had a travelling companion, Gudmundur Einarsson. Einarsson had come by Halifax, and for three years had gradually made his way across Canada and so could understand English. However, he was quite shy because of his accent and pretended he could not speak anything but Icelandic. As Gudmundur and Ketil watched the thickly wooded shore pass by, an Englishwoman and her husband came out of their cabin, and the Englishwoman said, "Do you think these are Icelanders?" Gudmundur translated for Ketil. The resulting exchange became a family story.

"I don't think so," the husband replied, shaking his head. "Icelanders are short and dark like Eskimos."

"No. No. There are a lot of Icelandic women working as domestics in Winnipeg. They wear those long black dresses and have blond hair."

"Swedes, I would think, or Germans."

"Ask them."

"Are you Icelanders?" he said, raising his voice.

"*Hvat?*" my great-grandfather asked.

The Englishman shouted, spacing out his words, "Are you Germans? *Deutsche?*" and pulled himself to attention and moved about as if he were marching.

"*Ert han vitless?*" Ketil asked Gudmundur.

"*Yow.*"

"I told you! That's their way of saying yes," the Englishwoman exclaimed. "I wrote to you about them. They had that terrible smallpox epidemic two years ago and they died like flies. The whole community was quarantined. No one allowed past Boundary Creek. When they let them back into Winnipeg, they didn't have a penny. You could hire them for nothing. Emma says they're excellent workers and clean. Another thing, they make their coffee in an old sock."

Coffee made in an old sock. I'd forgotten about that. It wasn't an old sock, actually. It was a linen bag sewed around a handle made of copper wire. The bag sat in the coffee all day. You just kept adding more grounds. And Ketil taking lump sugar between his teeth and sucking his coffee through it.

"But what did they call this old sock?" Helen asked when I told her about Ketil's story. "They must have had a name for it." She was always hunting for ethnic experience. Odd words, bits of information. Her previous boyfriend had been Russian and had given her a samovar and a marushka. She still made tea with the samovar. The boyfriend before that had been an Arab and had given her two Persian carpets she'd hung on her wall. She considered people with roots to be the most fortunate of creatures.

"I don't know. I probably never heard it. My mother was Irish. I was a half-breed."

Remembering was like digging up the dead, not whole people but bits and pieces, a fingerbone here, a vertebra there. Fragments of memory. Things forgotten or half-remembered. Eddyville, when I was a child, was still mostly swamp. People had built on the high ground, and the houses were separated by property that was never dry until the middle of summer. By then the grass would be head-high and the willows thick and tangled, the perfect place to play away from the prying eyes of adults. One day a dozen of us had been running the trails, playing cowboys and Indians, when we decided to build a fort we would call Valhalla. There was lumber we could steal from various yards and old blankets for a floor. Here, we were to be vikings. We would bring food and soft drinks and comic books and organize raids upon neighbourhood gardens and fruit trees.

We dispersed, then returned with our loot. When we had all gathered, Clarence pushed me back and said, "You can't come to Valhalla."

I had pinched a pocket full of my father's nails and an old tablecloth.

"Why not?"

"You're not Icelandic."

"I am so."

"My mother says you're not. She says your mother is an *utlander*."

"She is not!" I shouted, enraged, and Clarence and his brothers and sisters all began to shout, "*Utlander. Utlander.*"

"She is not. She is not," I yelled back, but it did no good. The others took it up. *Utlander*. Foreigner, outsider, other than us. None of the English words do it justice. Not wanted, perhaps.

I remember that with absolute clarity. The bone-coloured grass, the clumps of willow, the yelling, my feeling of helpless rage. I remember the next day even more clearly because that was the day Ketil, still proud, still strong, his moustaches yellow from snuff, died on his living room floor. He had hoped, I'd heard him say to my father, to die in his boat or in a woman's bed, but somehow, it was better that he'd died in his beloved house. It still stands today, nothing special now that houses are two thousand, four thousand square feet, even in Eddyville. It is small, wood frame, sits on a basement. Although I've not been in it in thirty years, I know it exactly. Back door entrance at ground level, stairs up and stairs to basement. When I think of the basement, I shiver, because he kept his coffin there on two sawhorses. To keep the dust off, he covered it with a white sheet. Once when my father and I came, Ketil was polishing the brass handles.

Upstairs, the kitchen, with a table in one corner. Two chairs. A washstand with a basin and a pitcher of water. Cupboards, but the colours escape me. Then the living room, but this is vague, the furniture uncertain, a couch, a trilight lamp, a front door and two bedroom doors, but these are dark holes behind cloth curtains. This house was his palace. It was his solace for failed dreams. His plan to bring his mother and father to join him. To pay their fare, to build a place for them. He worked like a madman. Taking anything that came his way—cutting wood, carrying mail, fishing, working on the railway, but by the time he had saved their fare, his mother was dead from starvation and overwork and his father too ill to make the journey. His mother had been buried without a coffin. He sent his father money so that he could escape from the farmers' council. Then Ketil began to save for his property, for his house. He built it himself, sometimes buying the lumber a board at a time. He married and had three children and those children had children and those, too, had children. I was one of those, a great-grandchild of the *hreppsomagur.*

A month after Ketil's death, his son, my grandfather, died. With that, two generations were buried in Canadian soil. Each of them was an Icelander. The man from Snaefellsness, the son of the man from Snaefellsness. My father, the next in line, was only twenty-eight. He was the grandson of the man from Snaefellsness. Then there was me. I was not the great-grandson of the man from Snaefellsness. I was *utlander,* not Icelandic but not Canadian either. No one was Canadian in those days.

At school, we aped the English. We sang "God Save the King" at the end of every school day. We learned to recite proudly Kipling and Wordsworth and Shelley. And we were taught to forget.

"What was that I heard you speaking? Was that English? It wasn't, was it?" the grade one teacher demanded. And standing at the front of the class, she punctuated each word with the leather strap that always hung at the side of her desk. What, strap, was, strap, that, strap, until Clarence was screaming and crying and trying to pull away as she beat his hands red. Afterward, twisted in his desk, his voice a high-pitched whine of pain, he rocked back and forth.

We were taught no sagas. No eddas. No mention of Skarphedin or Njal, Iceland's greatest hero, nor Thingvellir, the site of the oldest parliament in the world, nor Yggdrasill, the tree upon which the world is held, nor Ragnarok, the day of doom. Instead, we memorized the names and dates of English kings and queens. It did no good, of course. When the summertime came and the Winnipeg campers opened up their cottages, they protectively shut their children behind fences, on verandahs. Even if we stood on the Eddyville dock wrapped in the union jack and recited sentimental poems about wattles and daffodils and wanting to be in England, there was no disguising our foreignness.

In Iceland, the passion for reading and writing had survived natural disaster and human cruelty. Even the *hreppsomagur* brought books to Canada. There was nothing greater than to be *skald*, writer. In Ketil's living room there were eight books in Icelandic. They were set on a small shelf above the couch, precisely where immigrants from other groups might have put an icon or a plaster saint. Unfortunately, in these books there were no instructions that would help him deal with Canada. The sagas and eddas dealt with family feuds, with honour and lineage. Nor did he have any practical experience. In Iceland he had never seen a forest, had only heard rumours of polar bears brought to land on drift ice. He had never eaten vegetables except potatoes and, until the day he died, refused all offers of vegetables with the words, "I don't eat grass."

Fishing is what the Icelanders knew and fishing is why they came to Manitoba. They tried other places, but they were fishermen and Lake Winnipeg was an inland ocean. Except it froze over in winter. They didn't know what to do about that, but they figured it out. They chopped a hole and put down nets with poles and then they invented a jigger that pulled nets under the ice. And they left home and went north for fall fishing and winter fishing and went still farther north for white fishing. And the women, if they didn't go north to cook for a gang of men, moved in together to save money on fuel and groceries and to keep each other company until the season was over. When Ketil arrived, the settlers were fishing for food, but a market soon developed in Winnipeg and from Winnipeg to Chicago.

Having arrived with nothing, they had nothing with which to buy equipment, but the fish companies, financed by Americans, were eager to lend them whatever they needed. Before the season began, each fisherman would go to Winnipeg, cap in hand. I need a new set of nets, he'd say, and the company owner would say, and corks and leads and bridles? And the fisherman would add, I'll need credit for fuel, and the owner would say, and groceries for yourself and your family and how many men? And northwesters and woollen mittens and socks, the fisherman would say, and the owners would say, just remember you sell your fish to us and nobody else. Ketil borrowed from us but sold his fish to someone else. There's no credit for him. Not here. Not anywhere. You tell him that. You tell him he'll have to find some other work than fishing. And he did. He became a dairyman. He considered himself to be well out of it because when a fisherman came back after two months of shipping his fish to Winnipeg, the company informed him of the price they'd pay him. A cent a pound, two cents a pound, whatever they felt like. If he protested, there was no credit next year. Many years, a fisherman worked all season and owed more at the end than when he began. And their wives, our mothers, the ones who were brave enough, that is, would go to the hotel door and demand that the waiters send their husbands out so they could get part of the cheque to buy groceries and school clothes and a new dress and something decent for the house, and often what they got was a black eye.

Three days of Icelandic Celebration didn't leave much. And then it'd be grovelling to the company for more credit and the women helping each other out and making do. It was the women who persevered, who held everything together, who pushed their children through school and away to the city, to university if humanly possible. My mother was one of those.

"I've arranged for you to go to Winnipeg to stay with your grandmother," my mother said the August after I'd finished high school.

"I don't want to go to Winnipeg," I replied. "I'm getting a boat and going fishing."

"I've taken my knitting money and given it to your grandmother. It will pay for your tuition to United College."

"You can't do this," I protested. Her knitting money had been saved for years to buy a dining room suite.

"Your grandmother will keep you for no charge. I've got work for one day a week at the fish packers. I get five dollars a day. I'll give you that. You'll have to find the rest yourself. Your uncle says he can get you a job as a bus boy on the weekends at Eaton's."

"I'm going fishing with Dad. The company is going to give me credit."

"If you do well, there are some scholarships for Icelandic Canadians. They're all in *Logberg*."

"Icelanders are fishermen."

"Not in the West End of Winnipeg. If you go to First Lutheran, you'll meet Icelanders who work in an office and get their fish from the store."

"I'm not clearing dishes in Eaton's."

"Signy Eaton is Icelandic. It'll get you a job, but it won't keep it for you. Remember that."

And that was that. I was off to Winnipeg a week later and sitting at the back of the class, arms crossed, listening to truth and beauty when I wanted to be ripping the guts out of fish, chopping off their heads and getting drunk in the Eddyville parlour and dancing polkas to Johnny and His Musical Mates and getting laid in the back seat of the car outside the Eddyville community hall, but by the time I managed to get back to fishing in the spring it was too late. I didn't belong any more. At the beer parlour, when I sat down, everyone got quiet. It was like the minister had arrived. They were talking outboard motors and dirty nets and lousy fish inspectors, and when they asked me what I was learning and I tried to tell them about Rousseau or Hobbes or Shakespeare, it was like I was showing off. I tried a couple more times but it was no good, and after that I didn't go back.

"Axel!" Helen said.

"What?"

"We came out for a walk. You've been standing there for five minutes staring across the marsh. Ever since you got that call from Iceland, you've been lost in a daze."

"No!" I said, brushing off a mosquito.

"Yesterday, at the ballet, you sat like you were mesmerized. I don't think you saw a thing."

"What?"

"Oh, God," she said, "I give up."

Icelandic horses invaded my dreams. Shaggy Icelandic

ponies, a long line of them climbing up a mountain of lava, black, convoluted, the horses outlined against the sky, short sturdy horses, with their shaggy manes, topping the crest and descending to a lava desert that went on as far as the horizon. *Hestur.* The word jumped unbidden into my mind. And with it the teacher screaming.

"What's that? What did you call them?"

And I whispered, "*Hestur.*" It was what my great-grandfather had always called his horse with the white blaze on its forehead.

"What did I tell you? What kind of word is that? Show me what a *hestur* is. Here, this picture. What is this? Well, speak up. I can't hear you."

"*Hestur.*" The word was as thin and faint as monofilament.

"It is not," she screamed. "It is a horse. Horse, you idiot. Class, here is a horse, and standing in front of the picture of a horse is an idiot. Hold out your hand!" She grabbed my wrist and dragged me to the desk, raised the strap above her shoulder.

"What is this?" she yelled, and when I wouldn't open my hand brought the strap down on my clenched fingers.

"A horse," I screamed. "A horse."

"Again."

"Horse."

"Again."

"Horse. Horse. Horse. Horse. Horse."

I woke up in a terrible panic. Although it was thirty-four years earlier that I had been beaten, my hands were so stiff and swollen that I could barely move them. It was as if I had stored not only the memory but the actual physical experience. I sat in bed, holding my hands in front of me. The pain was so intense that I did not dare touch the light switch.

"Let's have *panacooker*," Helen said a few days later. She'd been rummaging around my kitchen cupboards and had found a cookbook. She held it up so I could see the cover. "The Lutheran Ladies Aid. Eddyville. Are you going to take me there sometime?"

"Sure," I said.

"*Vinarterta* sounds interesting. And *asta bolur*." She flipped through the pages. "And rosettes with fresh whipped cream. And *hangikjot*." She couldn't make any sense out of the *k* and *j* together. "And *hardfisk*."

They used to make hardfish in Eddyville. They split saugers and small pickerel and hung them on wires above the fly line. They cured in the sun, curling as the skin shrank. I got a tapeworm that way. Stealing hardfish before it was ready, my cousin stealing butter from his mother's kitchen. Then we put the fish skin-side down on the sidewalk and pounded it with a hammer until the flesh softened and we could tear off strips and drag them through the butter.

"It stinks," I said.

"What does?"

"Hardfish. It smells like an outhouse on a hot day."

"*Skyr*," she said. "A milk product. That doesn't tell you much, does it? *Rullapilsa.* That sounds vile." She read the description. "A sheep's flank rolled tightly, boiled, pickled, then sliced thin and served on brown bread. Did you eat this stuff?"

"With half a loaf and a tilted cup, I got myself a friend." I replied, without thinking.

"What is that all about?" She was onto it in a flash.

"Nothing."

"Oh, come on. Don't be so chintzy with your life."

"It was a saying of my great-grandfather's. He got it from a book called *Havamal.*"

I'd probably have picked a fight with her for being so nosy, but just then the phone rang and Disa somebody-or-other's daughter said, "Did your airplane ticket arrive?"

"Yes, but . . ."

"That is good. Someone will meet you at the airport. We have a very nice apartment for you at the university. I look forward to seeing you."

And then she hung up. Icelanders are like that. Abrupt. Not much subtlety. No small talk. In the sagas they're always saying, "Now I'm going to kill you," or something similar, and then they proceed to do it.

"Wait," I yelled. "You can't do this to me. Wait. I can't, I can't."

"What?" Helen said.

"Iceland."

"You were yelling at Iceland?"

"It's hard to explain."

"You might as well go. You haven't been yourself for the last six weeks. I'll drop by and take care of your cat every day. I promise. I'll even water your plants. Just bring me back one of those Icelandic sweaters."

"They can't do this. They didn't want us and now they're going to shanghai me."

"The people who didn't want your family are all dead."

"No, they're not. If they were, I wouldn't dream about them every night."

"You've earned your way back."

"With a couple of books of stories? You would think it would cost more than that."

"*Skald.*"

"That's a bad burn."

"That's a writer. It is a title of honour. That's what they called you in their letter."

"You've been learning a lot."

"The flight from Winnipeg is a charter. It only takes five hours."

"You're one of them."

"You can't let her win."

"Exactly. She can't just phone up here..."

"Not her. The old bitch with the strap. You can't, you know. It's not over yet. Your great-grandfather couldn't go back. Your grandfather couldn't go back. You can go back for them."

"He wouldn't walk down the block. He wouldn't watch the *fjalkona* lay the wreath at the monument. He split wood on Icelandic Celebration. All day."

"It must have been hard. Staying away."

The phone started to ring again. I let it ring, five, six times, then I said, "That's her calling back. What am I going to say? Shit! I can't do this. It's too hard." And then I grabbed the phone in a rage. "*Yow!*" I shouted. "*Godan daginn. Thetta er Axel Borgfjord. Yow. Yow.* Goddamn you, goddamn you, yes I'm coming." But it wasn't her, it was a wrong number.

The Man from Snaefellsness:
Part Two

He was lying in the bathtub, fully clothed, wrapped in a comforter, desperately trying to fall asleep, when there was a knock on the door. Her name was Fjola, she said, and she wanted to buy him breakfast and interview him for a series of articles she was writing on Western-Icelanders. Although he hadn't slept for twenty-six hours and it was now ten-thirty in the morning, he let her take him to Nordic House, where she fed him lox and caviar on toast and four cups of coffee.

"How was your charter?" she asked. She had her note pad and two freshly sharpened pencils on the table.

"Booze and singsongs," he said.

"Icelandic songs?"

" 'Home on the Range,' 'Row Your Boat,' 'A Hundred Bottles of Beer on the Wall.' " He stopped.

"I don't know those," she said, scribbling down the names. She treated everything he said with great seriousness.

"Would you like me to sing them?"

She glanced nervously at the people eating their breakfasts and reading the foreign newspapers.

"You're famous in Canada?" she asked.

"In my home town. My fame reaches from the lake shore to the railway tracks on the west, from the Canadian Legion on the south to the government bridge on the north."

She stopped writing. "You must be very tired," she said. "Maybe you'd prefer to be interviewed later?" She put her pencil down.

She was slender, light, as if she had hollow bones, and her

blond hair was pulled to one side and fastened with a leather clip so that it fell over her left shoulder. She was young, he thought, maybe twenty-four or five, too pretty for her own good.

"No," he said. "Now's fine."

After she left, he stayed to have another cup of coffee. For the next two weeks he was on his own most of the time. There were some formal meetings and receptions, but the committee that had invited him had been true to its word. It expected nothing of him except that he learn everything he could about the country. And it was prepared to let him decide how to do that. It was, he thought, less an official visit than a paid vacation. Knowing how fraught with tensions, conflicts, hidden agendas the committees were that dealt with North American immigrant groups, he wondered what would surface, what price would be asked at some later date.

Since Fjola had got the information she wanted, he didn't expect to hear from her again, but she surprised him, calling him early, waking him into confusion and painfully bright sunlight. She had, she said, more questions for him. She had a picnic basket packed, and if he was willing to continue the interview, they could talk while she showed him the countryside.

The fields of wild lupine surprised him. He had lupine in his garden at home and had seen it growing wild in the mountains, but he had not expected it here, at least not in such profusion. They stopped for coffee and pastry. It made a false impression, he thought. This ocean of green and blue, this girl with her pale blond hair and eyes the colour of new cornflowers. Her hair reflected the sunlight so that her head seemed surrounded by a nimbus. She wore brown leather boots, a tailored brown skirt, a white blouse with a gold clip in the shape of a fish. Stylish and perfect, but he was in no danger because he'd never found Icelandic women attractive. Other men oohed and aahed over them—tall, blond, statuesque, Nordic—Hitler's perfect wives and mothers. Goering had come here, to Iceland, to praise them—the purest of the pure, the living genetic containers of the master race.

When they left the lupine, they entered hills splashed with green and yellow and red, but it was colour from mineral salts and rock. There was not a single blade of grass. Everything had been burned away including the soil itself. Here, they left the car and walked to boiling springs reeking of sulphur, the ground acid-yellow and brown, the clear water bubbling and hissing. The ground was brittle as thin ice, dangerous. Stay in my footsteps, she warned him. A single misstep could plunge the careless traveller into ankle-deep superheated water, scald the flesh from his bones.

As they travelled, he was constantly misinterpreting things, judging them on the basis of his own experience. When he'd seen a pipeline he'd assumed it was for oil, but it had been for thermal hot water. When he'd been coming in from Keflavik there'd been smoke in the distance, and he'd assumed the farmers were burning off their fields. It was steam rising through the crevices. The black soil wasn't soil at all, but vast fields of volcanic cinder, and the green crops, up close, were a thin layer of moss and lichen.

"What," he asked her, "do I have to be careful about?"

She shrugged, reassured him that whatever he did, he would be forgiven. "You are *Vestur-Islenzkur. Skald.*"

"Come on," he cajoled, "you know what people say about the tourists."

"Talking about yourself is worse than being the whore of the district," she admitted. "There's only two hundred and fifty thousand people. Everybody's related. You don't need to talk about yourself. Everyone will do it for you."

"How curious will they be about me?"

She laughed. "They'll discuss even the hair in your ears."

She had other warnings. Don't shift your knife and fork from hand to hand and don't ever eat with your fingers. Open-faced sandwiches are to be eaten with utensils. If you're offered salad, treat it like a condiment. It's so expensive that they don't eat it like Americans. She'd been an exchange student in California for a summer and knew about American habits. If you are offered salmon, don't eat more than one piece. If you are offered lamb, don't take a second helping. Don't say anything critical about what you see or hear. Wear suits and ties, not jeans. Americans wore jeans and were simultaneously envied and despised. Envied because they could afford them and despised for wearing them to inappropriate places. Decorum was important to

Icelanders. Except, he thought, when they got drunk. He'd seen them drunk. Then there was no decorum at all.

"Do you consider yourself an Icelander?" she asked, and he said no and she said why not and he said look at the daisies growing along the road, I didn't know you had daisies in Iceland.

On their way to Thingvellir, the road jogged around a large rock.

"*Huldafolk*," she said, glancing at him to see if he knew.

"They didn't emigrate," he replied. "There are no unwashed children in New Iceland."

"Maybe," she said quickly, "there was no need for superstition in America. Maybe people had more control over their lives."

At Thingvellir, she showed him the reforestation, the evergreens that some people said were defacing the countryside.

"What they don't understand," she said, with an impatient shrug of one shoulder, "is that this was all wooded during the landtaking. There were forests, but they cut them down and the sheep kept them from growing again. People get so used to deprivation that they think it is normal."

The trees were a surprise, but not as much of a surprise as the rows of brightly coloured tents of the campers or the steady procession of tour buses. It was not as if he'd expected Skarphedin or Glum or Flossi to appear, or even thickset farmers dressed in stockings and wide hats, but, somehow, here in Ultima Thule, the end of the inhabitable earth, he had not expected busloads of tourists in brightly coloured shorts and shirts. It was better when she took him to the booths where the *godar* had lived during their yearly assembly. There was not much to see. Moss-covered walls a few feet high, but at least he could imagine the men, gathered for the annual parliament, the Althing, parading back and forth, displaying their vanity while seeking revenge for real and imagined insults. Fjola had found a seat on one of the walls and sat with her hands twined around her knee.

"The first democracy in the world was here," she said. "The first parliament. They settled their court cases here, and the Lawspeaker read the law from the Lawrock." But later, when they stood on the bridge over the river, and he asked her about the drowning pool, she quickly turned away and said, "After the Reformation they were very cruel."

At noon, they were the only patrons in the Thingvellir restaurant. As they ate pink-fleshed trout and drank one–per cent pilsner, she said, "It was the church," coming back to his question. "They drowned women for infidelity."

"Not now, though," he said. A waiter in a black suit and bow tie brought him their bill. "I read where one-third of the children are born out of wedlock."

"They cut off the men's heads. But it didn't stop them."

"I'll bet it did," he said.

That night she took him to see a play. He had expected to visit a theatre. Instead, they drove into the countryside. She turned off the main road and followed a path into a set of hills, and when she said they were called the red hills, he remembered his dream, the one he'd had immediately after he'd been invited to Iceland, a dream of vikings and his kinsmen in battle. It had been a ferocious dream. The struggle had seemed to go on without end. He had hacked off arms and legs and heads, had been wounded time and again, until from his wounds flowed bloody streams. His father, his grandfather, his great-grandfather, his uncles, his cousins, had fought beside him, shoulder to shoulder. When he had wakened from the dream, he had been exhausted, deafened by the screaming, the hammering of steel on steel. Now, if he had been driving, he would have turned around, but Fjola pulled onto a piece of ground where some other cars were already parked. They got out and he gave her some *kronur* to pay for tickets. They walked for about fifty feet, rounded a hill, and came upon a young man who reached into a large wooden chest and handed them Icelandic blankets.

"What is this for?" he asked.

"We'll be glad of these later," she said, and he followed her through the red hills to a small clearing where a set of bleachers had been constructed. They chose a seat near the top and wrapped themselves in their blankets; then she gave him a drink of coffee from her thermos and a drink of schnapps from a bottle in her purse. Before them there was a small patch of even ground. A campfire burned. There was a single, stunted birch. The flat ground was surrounded by deeply fissured lava. Behind this was a series of hills.

Fjola touched his arm and he looked up. On the crest of a hill, a viking was standing with a spear. The similarity to the image in his first dream made him jerk his hand to his side as if to grab a sword. An elderly man carrying a large wooden cross on his back was emerging from one of the fissures. He threw the cross to the ground, put his hand on a stone altar, and began to speak.

"What is it?" Fjola whispered, and he realized he was fiercely gripping her arm just above the elbow. He let go and shook his head. A second actor appeared. "Are you well?" Fjola asked. When Axel nodded, she said, "This is Mordur. He is confronting his father for praying to the pagan gods and desecrating the cross. His father is trying to convince him to forget Christianity and to obtain revenge on his enemies."

Afterward they went to a restaurant for a drink and dessert, and she pulled up the sleeve of her sweater. Just above her elbow there was a bruise where he'd clutched her arm.

"You have very strong hands," she said.

"I'm sorry," he answered. "I didn't mean to hurt you."

"Maybe Mordur frightened you," she said, laughing at him.

"Ghosts," he said.

"So they have ghosts in America," she answered. "No *huldafolk* but ghosts."

"People die there, too."

"No cruelty. No drowning pools."

"No," he said, "no drowning pools." But he knew his answer was dishonest, evading the real question.

"They were always fighting, though?" she said. "We see it in the Western movies."

"Not in Canada."

"Canadians and Americans are the same, aren't they?" she asked, and he wondered if she were insulting him, deliberately paying him back for mentioning the drowning pool.

"All my life, I've been looking for something," he said. "Trying to find an answer. That is why I write." It was the answer to an earlier question.

"Maybe you'll find it here," she said, as she wrote down what he'd said.

"That'd take a bloody miracle," he answered. "I can't even get traditional food." He made a disparaging gesture with his hand. "This is all German and French."

"We don't need to eat ram's testicles any more. No more singed sheep's heads. No rotted shark. They used to catch deep-sea sharks and bury them for six months and dig them up and eat them."

"The Chinese eat chicken feet."

"If you eat shark fresh it can cause internal bleeding, even death. Did you know that?"

"They could have grown vegetables."

"They don't eat grass," she said, and he thought of his great-grandfather Ketil and his endless meals of porridge and his fish and potatoes. After sixty-seven years in Canada, he still had refused to eat salad. Dogmatic, narrow-minded, suspicious of change. But he hadn't minded sleeping with the foreign women who stayed in the cottages while their husbands worked in Winnipeg. He'd make his rounds selling fresh milk and stay for coffee and a little dessert. Like spice, he used to say, each one tastes different—pepper, cinnamon, chocolate—and pull at his moustaches with his thumb and forefinger. An old goat, one of the women had said, but that was because he'd never tried to get into her bed. At least that was the story.

The next day, Gudmundur, the chairman of the committee that had invited Axel, picked him up just after breakfast. He was to take him to see his great-grandfather's farm. The trip would take three days, so Axel had dressed in jeans and a black leather jacket, but then, remembering Fjola's warning, he changed into sports pants, a knitted vest, tweed jacket and tie. Gudmundur, when he arrived, was dressed in nearly identical clothes. He was a tall man with large hands and feet and that peculiarly Icelandic way of always looking at things with his head slightly tilted back as if he were constantly judging everything and finding it wanting.

At the edge of the city the asphalt roads gave way to gravel sprinkled with rocks as large as baseballs. Gudmundur drove straight ahead, the wheels battering the rocks aside or riding over them, his eyes fixed on various legendary points of interest. This, he said, pointing with one hand, is where there was a farm until one evening the farmer came in and said a fissure was opening at the gate. The fissure grew until it buried the farm and created this crater. Here, he said later, pointing to some cliffs, an outlaw used to live. In those days if you were outlawed any man could kill you without penalty. The Althing had no power. It would be like your Canadian courts pronouncing sentence, then leaving it up to the victim or the victim's family to carry it out.

They skirted Whalefjord. Gudmundur said they'd stop at the whaling section if there was a whale being flensed. We'll know it well in advance, he said, rolling down the window and sniffing the air, then rolling up the window. There was nothing except the wet, slightly bitter smell of ocean. Later, when he rolled down the window again, Axel knew there was a whale being flensed. There was no need to be told. The smell, although they were more than a mile away, was overwhelming, thick and oily and rotten.

They parked above the whaling station and walked down to a wall where some other tourists were taking pictures. A mixed group of Japanese and Icelandic workers had just begun to cut the whale apart. The flensing knives were like large steel-footed hockey sticks, and as the workers sliced, the white blubber streaked with red meat peeled away in thick layers, which were then cut in strips, hooked and dragged away. A tractor with a winch pulled at one side of the whale, while other workers split it down the centre. Near to Axel, an Icelander stopped work, pulled a stone from his belt and began to sharpen his flensing knife. Like sharpening a scythe, Axel thought. But that wasn't it, that wasn't the image. It wasn't Brueghel, domestic, agrarian, and he had to search for a moment until the word viking jumped into his mind. Blood and bone and steel and death and pride: his pride clear in the way he stood, slightly bent at the knees, intent on the razor-sharp blade, aware that he was being watched.

They stopped at a fisherman's hotel at Borganes, and Axel was impressed by the sign on the door that said "Out of your boots," and as if in testimony to the authority of the sign-writer, fifty pairs of boots were neatly lined up in the lobby. Gudmundur and he ate with a crowd of young men, many of whom Axel recognized. Not that he really knew them or their names, but there, he wanted to say, is a Thorsteinsson, a Magnusson, a Bjarnason, a Vopfjord.

After supper, Gudmundur took out a book and they held their own *vaka*. Each sat on a single bed facing the other while Gudmundur translated passages. The book, he explained, was written by Axel's great-great-uncle, who had been both a heavy drinker and notoriously litigious. He was always well prepared and won his cases. Like me, Axel said, quick to sue, but he also thought Gudmundur had to skip a lot of relatives before finding one who had accomplished something. Axel imagined him rummaging through the family records, through the archives, like an evaluator of antiques sifting through a box of junk, hoping to find something semiprecious, not a real antique but at least something collectible, not wanting to give up until he was able to assure the owner that there was something of value in his basement treasure trove.

All that day plus half the next day the mountains were barren, an icy chain rising on their right. On their left there was always the ocean. In the narrow space between, there was hay land, a green ribbon circling the country. Every so often, there was an isolated farm. They came, at last, upon what had seemed a mountain of smooth stone, but he'd learned to wait, to suspend judgement and comment, and he was glad he had not said how he'd like to climb its smooth sides because when they got close it was a mountain of gravel. Just beyond this was the farm of his great-grandfather. Not the farm his great-grandfather had owned but the farm that had owned his great-grandfather. It was a wonder, he thought, that *hreppsomagur* had not had their ears notched like the cattle and sheep. It was probably not compassion that kept the farmers from doing it; the welfare cases were of less value than the animals.

The visit to his great-grandfather's farm was to be the highlight of his trip, the epiphany, the moment when past and present were joined again, the circle completed. But it was not like that. He had not known what to expect, but somehow, fantastically, he had hoped to set things right, to obtain revenge, to undo injustice, somehow to drive his sword through the body of Ketil's enemy and even the balance with blood. As they drove, he brooded, still not certain that he should have come, if even now he should not return the trip's cost, pay for everything with his own silver. *Vergild*, he thought. They were paying him with *vergild*. They had asked him for nothing in return; the payment for his fare, for his apartment, the food, was for nothing in the present. It was reparation for past injustice.

The original house was gone. All that remained were a few piles of stones. Beside the tumbledown walls, there was a modern bungalow that needed painting. The farmer and his wife were getting ready to make hay, but when Gudmundur explained who Axel was, they went back inside to serve him coffee and cake. Axel had commented on four eagles' claws, and these, he was told, came from the old house. They had been preserved by smoke from the fireplace where they had hung for decades. Now, they hung beside an electric fireplace. He had expected something, but not this farmer sitting on a worn red couch, a window full of flowering geraniums, his wife shyly serving them coffee, obviously flattered but uncomfortable with city guests. There had not been another house for miles, and the television must have been a solace during the long winter. American soap operas replacing the *vaka*, the evenings spent reading the sagas or the Bible aloud. Later, he had walked the shingle beach, studied the narrow homefield where the hay was already partly cut and was lying out to dry, and the pretty lagoon. He'd have stayed longer, but it was a warm clear day and he knew he was keeping the couple from their work. Instead of fire and steel, he left a box of Rogers' chocolates. A mile down the road, Gudmundur stopped beside a graveyard. There was nothing fancy here, no angels, no sarcophagi, but only weathered headstones, a wire fence, some rough, patchy grass on the gravel.

"Your great-great-grandfather is buried here," Gudmundur said.

They found his stone. Axel knew its story. Ketil had paid for it, had also sent money for a headstone for his mother's grave, had paid for her to be dug up, for her bones to be placed in a coffin. Her headstone was beside her husband's. It had taken a year's savings for each stone. Three more years' savings for a casket and reinterment and graveside service. Even in the years before his death Ketil had fretted that he should have had his parents' bones brought to Canada, buried among friends, but he'd said, who was to tell that they would send the right ones.

They travelled back by way of the interior, over a narrow dirt road, past vast tracts of stone. They followed a river part way, but even here there was no growth, no lush banks of trees or shrubs, but clear, fast-running frigid water. When it seemed that no one else existed, when they had crossed over a vast rocky plain bounded by glaciers, they came upon a small country store and stopped. There was a car parked outside, and to his amazement, when they went in, there were two women wearing T-shirts that said: "We're from Arkansas and proud of it." Their children were squabbling loudly over American chocolate bars, and one of their husbands was warning the others to buy plenty of soft drinks and snack foods because who knew how soon they would find some-place where they could buy real food again. The criticism nettled Axel, as if it were him they belittled with their comments, and he had to remind himself that this was not his country, that his fam-ily was *hreppsomagur*, that he was *utlander*. And yet when one of the men turned to Axel and asked him what the name of this godforsaken place was, Axel shrugged his shoulders and said, "*Hvat? Tala thu Islenzku?*"

When he returned to his apartment, there was a message from Fjola. "I will take you to see miracles," it said.

By the time she arrived, rain was pouring down, blurring everything, and he wondered if they shouldn't spend the day at his apartment where it was dry and comfortable and safe, but she was determined to make the journey.

"What did you learn?" she asked.

"That there's a lot of rock in Iceland," he said.

Because of the rain, she wore a wide-brimmed, waterproof hat and a tan raincoat. She'd braided her hair so that it hung down her back. The hat was too big, she'd borrowed it, and it made her look even younger, more innocent, like an inexperienced angel.

They began at Skaholt, the oldest bishopric in Iceland. Once, it had been the centre of power, a cluster of buildings around the largest stave church in Europe, a centre of intrigue and wealth. Now it was reduced to a cathedral and a manse. The cathedral was locked, but Fjola obtained a key from the manse. Inside, it was white, plain, starkly Lutheran, only the mosaic of Christ be-hind the altar glowing with colour. A busload of tourists arrived. As they trooped through the door, noisy, pointing, taking pictures in spite of the sign that forbade it, Fjola unlocked a door, shepherded Axel ahead of her and, after firmly shutting the door behind her so no one could follow, led him down a staircase to a stone coffin enclosed in glass.

"This bishop's coffin is described in one of the sagas," she ex-plained. "No one believed it actually existed. When they were excavating for the new cathedral, they discovered it."

"The Lord works in mysterious ways," he said.

They avoided the tourists by leaving through an old tunnel, which had also been discovered during the excavation and had been reconstructed. As they drove away, he asked about a small monument enclosed by a chain fence.

"It is the grave of the last Catholic bishop of Iceland and two of his nine sons," she said. "They were beheaded for being nationalists."

Then they had gone to Gullfoss. Here the double falls thundered into a narrow gorge. Gullfoss was greater than Niagara, more spectacular for being contained, the falls dropping into a milk-white maelstrom. The force was so great that water was driven back up into the air like rain defying gravity. The ground close to the edge was smooth with mineral deposits. Axel walked away from Fjola, approached the edge and stared at the endlessly violent water. He might have become mesmerized but for the endless coming and going of the tourists, their cameras out, their umbrellas hoisted.

From there they fled to Geysir. "It used to be a miracle," she said. "People came from around the world to see it spout, but it stopped working so they used to put dish soap into it. Now, even that does not help."

A large basin from which wisps of steam curled was all that remained. One of the smaller geysers erupted, shooting into the air in a white jet, the spray breaking, falling in a rain that sent the tourists running backward. Another tour bus stopped and a soccer team tumbled out. They were very drunk, some of them holding bottles of Black Death. They were yelling, not at anyone or anything, but drunken, mindless yelling that comes before passing out.

"Danes," Fjola said contemptuously, as she led him back to her car.

"I thought Scandinavians were all the same," he said, "like Americans and Canadians."

"That's not funny," she said, and she did not talk to him until the silence had become brittle, as though they were lovers who had quarrelled. "You are not stupid," she said. "You know what the Danes did to Iceland."

"It was a long time ago," he said. "Let bygones be bygones."

Her face tightened, and he thought that if she was not so polite she would have made him get out of the car. He wondered how he would find his own way back. As far as he could see in any direction, there was only lava and rock. He could walk for hours and not find another human being. He handed her his mickey of Black Velvet, but she refused it with the excuse that she was driving.

"*Hreppsomagur*," he said.

"They did it everywhere," she said. "Scotland. England."

He realized he was bullyragging her, but he couldn't stop, couldn't quit choking on a rusted hook stuck in his throat. "No wonder you always talk about sagas," he said, with a bitterness that surprised him. "Remember the sagas. Nobody wants to talk about later."

She wouldn't cry. He knew that. He wondered if they ever cried. Maybe when they were alone and the door locked. The men never cried. It wasn't allowed. That was one of the taboos. Men must never show feminine characteristics. Women must never show male characteristics. If they did, they were mocked and humiliated until they followed the rules. Even if teachers beat the language out of you, you still had to follow the rules. One of the men in Eddyville had had a tartar of a wife. She bossed him about endlessly, and, one day when his friends dragged him into the parlour, his wife went in and dragged him out; the day after that, he climbed up on the wagon he normally used to haul garbage for the town and shot himself in the face with a shotgun.

He didn't expect her to stop the car again. She'd drive him back to his apartment and that would be the end of her. He'd never see her again. He hadn't asked her to show him around, hadn't tried to get her into bed, hadn't wanted anything from her, he thought, with a rage that made him want to pound on the dashboard, smash the windows.

They were approaching a cluster of houses when steam began to pour from the hood of the car. She slowed, pulled off the highway and coasted down a side road, then stopped. They got out together and lifted up the hood. Steam billowed around them.

"What's wrong?" she asked, bewildered. "I just had it checked."

"I don't know," he said. "I'm not good with mechanical

things." But he did spot the broken fan belt caught on the motor.

She took the belt from him and went to a nearby house. When she came back, she got into the car and told him that someone was bringing another belt from the nearest garage.

The rain had turned to a steady drizzle. She's run out of miracles, he thought, and took another drink. No cathedrals, no monuments, no natural wonders. Just a piece of unkempt grass surrounded by a fallen-down fence, then a beach and two over-turned boats. One red, one blue.

A tiny stream, no more than a foot across, rising from a spring, crossed the lot, which was about half the size of a suburban yard. The stream split to make a rough circle, joined again, then ran out of the field, across the beach, past the two overturned skiffs, into the lake. Without inviting him to come, she got out and stepped over the fence and walked to the stream. He put the cap back on the whiskey bottle and followed her. The whiskey was beginning to affect him, and he stumbled slightly. She had stopped where one of the branches of the stream formed a pool just large enough for someone to sit in if they pulled their knees to their chest.

She squatted and dipped both hands into the water. "They brought their bodies here," she said, "after they'd beheaded them. They laid them out and washed them for burial."

There was no one else, no one on the beach, no one on the road, no sign of anyone coming or going from the houses, which looked shut against the rain. He thought that was all, that whatever she wanted to say had been said, but she lingered, the rain gathering on the wide brim, running in a trickle onto her back.

"When the Icelanders decided to become Christian at a meeting of the Althing, they could have been baptized at Thingvellir, but the water there was glacial. This water comes from a hot spring. They accepted Christ here."

"It didn't make them behave any better," he said.

"Some," she said in a clipped voice. "Some were better." She went back to the car.

Axel took a plastic bag out of his pocket. He put it down, then knelt on it. He hesitated, then cupped his hands in the water. The water was warm, and he realized how cold his hands had been. Numb. Nearly as sore at first as when, as a kid, he'd frozen them while playing hockey and his mother had put them in a basin of warm water. In the name of the Father, Son and Holy Ghost, as it was in the beginning and ever shall be, he thought, and wondered if that was right.

Kneeling there, he remembered Ketil. His enemies were all dead, he thought. What is a man to do when he finally returns and the enemy is all dead, and crazily he remembered a news item about a Japanese soldier who had stayed in the jungle for thirty years out of loyalty to the emperor, fighting a war that didn't exist. He went to get up and couldn't and thought it was the whiskey, but it wasn't that, it was as though his body were swollen, distorted, clumsy, as if he had some terrible disease that had covered him with tumours, and he felt as if he were a supplicant praying that he be made well, and when he struggled to his feet, he slipped, and one leg plunged into the water, which rose just past his knee and he knew what he had to do. He hesitated, wondering what she would think, then dragged his other leg after him, awkwardly, as if it had fallen asleep, and sat down in his hundred-dollar pants and his raincoat and pulled his knees to his chest and bent his face to the water.

Forgive me as I forgive those who trespass against me. The thought came unbidden, slipped out, and he thought that when she told others about what he had done they would talk about it for years, for his lifetime, even after his death, the crazy writer, the great-grandson of the *hreppsomagur* from Snaefellsness, who sat in the baptismal pool in his good clothes. And if they were generous, they would say that he'd had too much to drink and had stumbled and fallen, but he no longer cared.

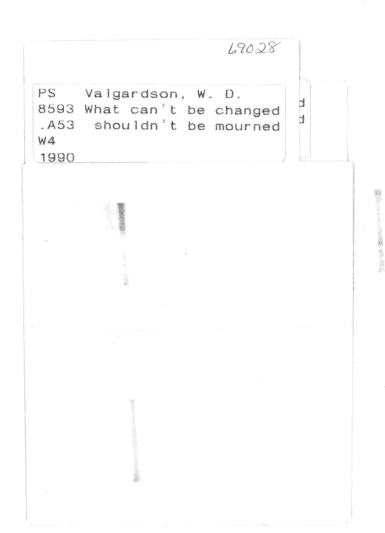